Responsible Adults

Praise for
Patricia Ann McNair

Responsible Adults

"*Responsible Adults* is devastating, in the best possible way. McNair guides us through domestic worlds where we might fear to tread alone, revealing truths and exposing worlds peopled with want, kitchens with empty refrigerators and strange men. Children eat grape jelly with a spoon and long for ordinary lives as they negotiate adult problems as best they can. Readers are wiser and more compassionate for knowing these stories."

—Bonnie Jo Campbell, author of *American Salvage*
National Book Award finalist

"In her piercing collection, Patricia Ann McNair confronts those charged with caring and protecting us, and who are—indelibly—responsible for what we become. The stories in *Responsible Adults* pull at the tether that winds from children to their parents, from wife to husband, from sister to brother, from stranger to stranger—always, it seems, on the verge of snapping. A young daughter charts the unsuccessful, often abusive, dating life of her widowed mother; an adult son perpetually listens for his father's voice inside a can of beans; a daughter communicates her pain through messages on her estranged father's answering machine; a substitute teacher tries to connect with a grieving student; a widowed minister takes in a young and pregnant stranger. In a small Midwestern town, McNair's characters teeter between absence and yearning, stagnancy and change. Always, she treats them with compassion and care. *Responsible Adults* is bursting with gorgeous, gutting stories."

—Sahar Mustafah, author of *The Beauty of Your Face*

"Patricia Ann McNair's *Responsible Adults* is a journey to a land where adults have let their wounds define them, forcing the children to become their own heroes. I read this gripping collection with my seatbelt tight, barreling from desperation to hope, danger to redemption, struggle to peace. There are writers who allow you to keep a safe distance from the lives of their characters. And there are writers like McNair, whose stories fly so low to the truth, you are thankful you can read them safely from 30,000 feet."

—Desiree Cooper, author of *Know the Mother*
Pulitzer Prize nominated journalist

"With startling honesty, precise observation, and a deep faith in the beauty of language, Patricia Ann McNair creates a world where the so-called adults in the room abandon, lie, cheat, steal. They're familiar, these faults, you think as McNair traces the delicate cracks and gaping chasms of the human condition, her gaze unflinching, unnerving, watching as opposing forces collide, unleash catastrophe. Especially then. Who, she seems to ask, is left behind and why turn away? In this remarkable collection, McNair hits her writerly stride with a sureness that is nothing less than breathtaking."

—Christine Maul Rice, author of *Swarm Theory*

"Have you ever read a book with characters so real, so present, it feels like they're in the same room with you? It's a feat of alchemical magic and McNair is the sorceress here. In these pages, you'll lock eyes with people on the margins, bent and bloodied—but not broken, never broken. You know who these people are. You see them on the street, at your job, out your window, and in your mirror."

—Giano Cromley, author of *What We Build Upon the Ruins*
and *The Last Good Halloween*

"In this devastating collection, McNair's stories deftly untangle the precarious cords of intimacy, revealing how the deepest of injuries are inflicted. Teeming with accidents and absence and cut-throat consequences, McNair's struggling adults are not enough and too late, and vulnerable children are resilient and resourceful by necessity. In gripping, aching prose, soda spills and ruins shirts, cars crash in reverse, voicemails pile up, names are scratched in frost, families split in an instant, irrevocably. These stories are not alarming because they're dangerous, they're alarming because they're familiar. This is one hyper-perceptive, fiercely honest, heart-expanding collection."

—Kate Wisel, author of *Driving in Cars with Homeless Men*
Drue Heinz Literature Prize winner

"The compression of the prose, its honesty and quiet intensity, earmarks a voice I find in Patricia Ann McNair's *Responsible Adults* to be mesmerizing, irresistible, a graceful on-key edginess that propels each story forward. If justice were served, this collection would stand among the best as reason enough to increase the readership for short fiction. It delivers that kind of punch, compassion, and staying power."

—Jack Driscoll, author of *The Goat Fish and the Lover's Knot*

And These Are the Good Times
finalist, Montaigne Medal, Eric Hoffer Awards

"Short story writer McNair . . . proves to be an irresistible personal essayist of refreshing candor, vibrant openheartedness, rueful humor, and unassuming wisdom . . . vital, confiding, potent, and superbly well-crafted essays."

—*Booklist*

"McNair's essays are challenging, colloquial, and contemplative. Her work recalls Jo Ann Beard and Mary Karr in its powerful insistence and range."

—Joe Meno, author of *Marvel and a Wonder*

"The essays in *And These Are the Good Times* are so arrestingly good that I had to stop several times to marvel at how keen, generous, and compassionate Patricia McNair's writing is. She's put her arms around the world and embraced so many of its complexities with the great heart and wondering eye of a poet."

—Christine Sneed, author of *Little Known Facts*

The Temple of Air
Chicago Writers Association Book of the Year
Southern Illinois University Devil's Kitchen Readers Award

"McNair's plainspoken yet imaginative, complexly unnerving, and haunting stories raise essential questions of fate and will, appearances and truth, guilt and compassion."

—Donna Seaman, *Booklist*

"The stories in *The Temple of Air* are steeped in a particular brand of hospitality and violence. They are definitively Midwestern, navigating deftly between the everyday and the disturbing, the prosaic and the poetic."

—*New City*

"Stunning debut collection."

—*TheNervousBreakdown.com*

"*The Temple of Air* is a book of unusual pleasures, each story offers the reader a small roller coaster of anticipation, fear, surprise, recognition, satisfaction. This is a beautiful book, intense and original."

—Audrey Niffenegger, author of *The Time Traveler's Wife*

"These stories speak to us in voices that are clear, urgent, tough, and shockingly wise. Patricia Ann McNair's *The Temple of Air* is about the spiritual resilience of endangered children, the survival methods of battered adults, and the presence of grace even in our ruined century."

—David Huddle, author of *The Story of a Million Years*

"Fiercely imagined, emotionally charged, Patricia Ann McNair's first collection celebrates the extraordinary potential of ordinary lives in ways that will leave you breathless."

—A. Manette Ansay, author of *Good Things I Wish You*

"These are lyrical stories that sear themselves into the reader's subconscious, and we are incredibly lucky that Patricia Ann McNair has written them. I can't wait to read more."

—John McNally, author of *After the Workshop*

Responsible Adults

Stories by

Patricia Ann McNair

Cornerstone Press
Stevens Point, Wisconsin

Cornerstone Press, Stevens Point, Wisconsin 54481
Copyright © 2020 Patricia Ann McNair
www.uwsp.edu/cornerstone

Printed in the United States of America.

Library of Congress Control Number: 2020942116
ISBN: 978-1-7333086-4-9

Cornerstone Press titles are produced in courses and internships offered by the Department of English at the University of Wisconsin–Stevens Point.

DIRECTOR & PUBLISHER   EXECUTIVE EDITOR   DEVELOPMENT COORDINATOR
Dr. Ross K. Tangedal   Jeff Snowbarger   Alexis Neeley

SENIOR PRESS ASSISTANTS
Brendan Gallert, Johanna Honore, Heidi Propson, Aleesha Splinter, Brianna Stumpner

SUMMER/FALL 2020 STAFF
Colin Aspinall, Colton Bahr, Shelby Ballweg, Seth Barnes, Kala Buttke, Ryan Condon, Tucker De Guelle, Andrew Eisele, Amber Elsworth, Ava Freeman, Morgan Frostman, Sid Hart, Claire Hoenecke, Nichole Hougard, Amy Jordan, Aya Kacprzynski, George Klumb, Jacob Maczuzak, Gavrielle McClung, Kiera Meidenbauer, Dylan Morey, James Paul, Katelyn Pietroske, Abigail Shortell, Tara Sparbel, Katelyn Voorhies

For the men I've lost: Wilbur, Roger, Paul
And for the one I found: Philip

Also by Patricia Ann McNair:

The Temple of Air

And These Are the Good Times

Contents

What Was To Come

Dorothy lost her mother.

They were out in the night; she wandered off.

It wasn't the first time. They'd be sitting on kitchen chairs in the yard telling stories—Ma had eighty-some years of them—and she'd stand up, shaky on a hip that didn't work much anymore.

"A minute," she'd say. "Be right back." And usually she would be. After a walk in the woods. A squat and a pee.

This time though, Dorothy'd lost her.

"Ma," she called into the dark. "Ma?"

She heard it then: what was to come soon enough. Any day now. The grief. The loss.

"Ma?"

My Mother's Daughter

My mother was a toucher. She tapped her fingers on my wrist, and even though I was sixteen, not really a girl anymore, I loved it, the feel of her pink touch. Such small hands. You couldn't help but notice.

I was my mother's daughter so I was not small, but she treated me like I was, especially when we sat, quiet like that. Waiting. The smell of spaghetti sauce still in the air, a little burned since she'd left it on the stove too long. He said he'd be here by midnight. He promised, she said. It was 11:50 and outside, headlights went by in columns in the dark. Lots at first as the summer sun dropped, then fewer, fewer.

He'd called—when? Seven or so I guess, an hour past when he first said he'd come. Work, he said. Mom believed him.

He wanted to meet me, she told me. They'd had three dates. Met at the diner after her shift. And he loved her little hands, he'd said. The way her fingers curled around the handle of the coffee mug. The way she used them to brush the bangs from her eyes, wipe the rings of mascara out from the creases there.

She'd woken me up then, that night when they'd first met. Come into my room and sat on my bed which rocked and dipped when she sat. (She used to be small. Sparrow small. I saw it in her old pictures. I know that it's true.)

And I was up, just like that, sitting and blinking in the dark.

"What? What?"

"It's me, Baby," Mom said. "Mommy. Shh now." And she smelled like the cigarettes she smoked in the backyard after sunset—smoking towards the sky, clouds towards the stars.

"I've met someone," she said.

"Oh," I said. What I did not say: "Again?"

So on this other night, the one when he was supposed to meet me, we sat on the couch that still had cat hairs in its cushions even though Shanty, our cat—my cat—had run away four months before. It was early summer hot, and we sat there in shorts and tank tops, hiding nothing. And I could tell that my mom was in need; her tiny hands made a ring around my wrist, and she hummed, like she would. A distraction. She did it when she was afraid, like when we were driving on the interstate after my grandfather died and the sun was hours from up and the gas light was on and the car made some rattle noise and there was nothing around but fields of night, and deer dead on the side of the road. She hummed while she ate. And she did it when she was anxious, this humming. Like when she waited in the dentist's office every six months, her pink cupid's bow lips vibrating. My mother had beautiful teeth.

Small hands and beautiful teeth. And a face so pretty that when we'd stop at a red light men stared at her poised at the wheel, men in trucks and cars and just walking by. A head turner, my grandfather—her dad—used to say. He said it up until the day he died, there in the hospital, while she sat next to his bed, holding his big hands in her little ones. Me down the hall getting a Pepsi from the machine. And I wished it could always be that way, my mother making heads turn with her prettiness, her lovely smile, her eyes, her long neck.

But, and it kills me to tell you this, I feel guilty even just saying it, that's all she's got really. A pretty face. A long neck. Small hands. Beautiful teeth. The rest of her is something else, something big and scarred. Scarred from when she ran into a tree one afternoon, that day when I was—what? Two?—and she and my dad (I never knew him, unless you count him living with us before I understood what knowing people meant, what it felt like to know someone, to see them, recognize them, yearn for them) were out on the highway coming home from her work, where he'd always pick her up because she didn't used to know how to drive, and he didn't used to want her to. She told me all this later when she wanted to talk about it. Later, when I was older, a few years ago, when I started to ask.

Her pretty face and delicate, soft hands and pink lips and shiny smile were all I got to see of my mother back then. I mean, I knew she was big (all right, I'll say it even though it sounds mean—she was fat) but she mostly stayed covered up in long, flowy blouses with sleeves all the way down to her wrists, and pants with wide legs to the tops of her shoes. Didn't matter if it was winter or summer, she'd wear pretty much the same thing all the time. I mean, not the exact same thing, she had dozens of these blouses, these fancy pants in her closet in all kinds of colors, dark mostly, and rich. Jewel colors, she called them.

This next thing happened when I was ten. We were in the backyard, and it was summertime. Mom held an unlit cigarette in her fingers, trying to quit, she said; no will-power she said. And up and down the block people were in their yards, fences and trees and imaginary boundaries separating us from one another even though we waved and called out and sometimes crossed onto someone else's lawn, to chase a ball maybe, or to tell a story. It was a nice neighborhood, not the best in town, but good. Families, and men who had jobs and places to go during the day, and women who hung wash on the line when the weather was nice. Not like where we used to live before we got that money from grandpa's insurance, in an apartment with mice and a living room window that faced an alley. And so we were out there in our yard sitting in the low, long lawn chairs Mom had bought on her latest paycheck day, their plastic seats slippery with sweat, their armrests too hot under the sun. But we didn't care. It was summer. School was done and the rain that always seems to soak our spring, had finally stopped. Things smelled green and new, and the neighbors who had gardens were out there digging in their flowerbeds, and the cicadas buzzed and the dog down the street barked a little and Shanty stretched in the cool grass under my chair and sipped at the air with her little pink nose and some kids a couple of houses over splashed and squealed in a wading pool.

And then my mom screams and tries to jump up from her chair. Only she can't quite, because her sleeve gets hooked on the armrest, and she gets all tangled for a minute and goes over in the grass, her shirt torn and her beautiful teeth showing like a snarl. And I'm there at her side in a blink, reaching for her, but she pushes my hands away, not mean, just sort of insistent. And she's dropped the cigarette and she's pulling at her blouse, tugging it up and away from her skin and up over her head. "A wasp," I hear her say, muffled in the shirt, and I see how her skin on her belly is tight and shiny—it looks like (I've thought about this a lot since then) melted and stretched cheese, kind of bubbly and pulled. And why haven't I ever seen this before, I wonder. I mean, have I never seen my mother's tummy before? But I can't remember having ever, so maybe I haven't. Maybe this strange stretched skin isn't something new like I thought at first it might be; and I swat at the wasp that has left his mark on my mother, a bright red blotch on her shiny cheese belly. And Shanty is up and batting at it, but the wasp just bobs in the air and lazily—probably so full of blood (do they do that, wasps? Drink your blood like mosquitoes?) that it is hard to gather any steam—flies off toward the house next door with Shanty, long and ropy, running in the grass behind it. And my mother is crying. But it doesn't sound like hurt crying, like pain crying. She is weeping like she has lost something really important, and maybe she has, I don't know, and she pulls on the hem of her blouse to cover up her cheesy stomach and stays in the grass with her arm over her eyes. And the torn sleeve shows that there is more stretched cheese-skin on her arm, curling over and around her elbow.

"Does it hurt?" I ask her, and I'm up close, kneeling in the grass so she can hear me and I don't have to talk too loud. "Does it hurt?" I say again, only I don't know if I mean the place where the wasp stung her or if I mean something else, her shiny, tight skin, maybe, or what it must feel like for her to understand that what I know now is not what I thought I knew before. And that she will have to tell me everything.

My father drove like a crazy man. Speeding and taking corners like a driver in the movies or on a cop show. Always. But especially when he was mad. Something set him off, my mom remembers and tells me, when he'd come for her that day at the school where she worked in the cafeteria. "He saw me talking to one of the building guys, I can't even remember his name now, something different, foreign, Rajid? Ramon? I think he said, *nice day*, or *have a good weekend*, or *see you tomorrow*. That's it, but I guess I smiled at him, and your father was nuts about my smile, so whenever I smiled at anyone else, he'd flip. *What was that about? Who you smiling at? Friend of yours?* That kind of thing. *No*, I'd say. *Was I smiling?* And I'd apologize. I was so young. I didn't know anything."

We were back in the kitchen now and Shanty was on the counter, her gold eyes on us at the table, tail switching. Mom had made a mixture of baking soda and water, was dabbing it on the red sting with a cotton ball and hissing through her lovely teeth. She was in nothing but her bra and slacks, and I could see it all. The crazy white scars and so much skin the color of a flesh crayon. Her face was scraped a little from the grass, I think, and there was mud on the knees of her pants. I rested my cheek on the cool Formica tabletop and watched her sideways. Listening. Not wanting to know, but needing to.

"He always took the backroads to our house from the school." We used to live in a trailer in the woods on the edge of town. I don't remember it, but I've seen it, too, in a picture. Blue. Sky-colored. With a pretty little flower bed and a knee-high white fence around it. My dad's in that picture, too, with dark hair and a straight, tight mouth, and glasses that caught the sun in them. Tough. Mean, maybe. And my mom is holding his hand, and has her other pretty little hand on his arm. She's a stick then, except for the balloon under her yellow dress that she told me was me. And she'd always told me—when I'd asked—that my dad had died, an accident, she'd said, but this was the first time—this time when I was ten—that she told me everything else.

I imagined the car (a big old mustard-colored Buick, also in the picture) hurtling over the gravel roads, hitting the rises and lifting up a little before slamming back down, my mom and dad feeling it all in their stomachs, in their backs. There's always that sweet, empty floating thing in your belly when you crest a hill and just before you sail downward; but then there's that bang at the base of your spine when you hit bottom. I wonder if my mom screamed then, yelled at him to slow down, cut it out, relax. The mom I knew was never much of a yeller. So I doubt she did; instead she probably held fast to the seatbelt, pushed a delicate hand up to the car's ceiling, clawed at the felt of it, and pulled her pretty, pink lips closed over her pretty, perfect teeth, holding on.

"There was a tree at the T in the road where we made our turn," she told me, "the only one out there in the fields, a half-mile from where the woods started up for real. I loved that tree. It must have been at least a hundred, as big around as it was. And in the fall it went bright red. And its leaves hung on for just about ever until they dropped, all at once it seemed like, and then those big bare branches made shapes in the sky. Like art. It took my breath sometimes." Mom went to the sink to empty the little cup of baking soda salve and wash her small hands. The flesh of her arms shook. She looked at the blank wall, like maybe there should be a window there, something to see, but there wasn't. "He was going too fast for the turn. He had to know. He had to."

She didn't remember the crash or the fire or those few weeks in the hospital. She remembered some things, though. The sound of my father wailing. The smell of burned rubber and something else, sweet and meaty. She remembered my grandfather coming to pick her up from the hospital with me in my car seat; she remembered weeping at the sight of me, even though—I'm told—my diaper was full and stinking. She remembered weeping, too, when they passed the tree on the way to our trailer and she saw the trunk burned black and scarred, its bark pulled away like a scab. She remembered telling me for the first time that same evening that my father had died—but I was only two and didn't get it or didn't care—and her feeling relieved that it didn't seem to matter to me one way or the other. She remembered the taste of rice pudding, the only thing she would eat for weeks, and how now she couldn't even bear to look at it, slimy and pebbly and milky in the bowl. She remembered waking up in the dark for a long time after, months, maybe years, with her skin still burning and her heart aching and wanting—not my father, because she knew, like she might have known all along, that he was not a good man, not a man worth wanting—but wanting to not be alone.

We didn't talk about this after that summer day with the wasp, but it was always there. My mother stopped hiding her scars from me, even though she still hid them from the rest of the world as best she could under her blouses, her pants. But whenever we sat at that kitchen table where she'd told me everything, we rarely talked anymore. Instead we filled our plates over and over and ate every bit of whatever we had, filling in the spaces left over from the story, left over from the crash.

I was skinny before that ten-year-old summer, my mother's daughter like I said, but up until then, I was like my mother the stick. But then I got to be something other than stick-like, no longer flat (*as a board,* the kids said, *as a pancake*), but rounder and filling out. It was a sudden change, I guess, so people noticed.

By the time I was thirteen I didn't really fit into little girl clothes anymore. Once at Sears shopping for school, we tucked into the narrow dressing room that smelled like sweat and feet, and my mother gave me a ladies' blouse, with darts and tucks. And the skirts from the juniors department hugged my hips too tight—even the ones for the chubbies. And I can remember my mom sitting behind me on a stool while I tried things on, and she was crying. "You're growing up," she said to me when I asked, but now I think it had more to do with me getting fat, not grown. "You're not fat," Mom would say when I worried out loud. But I figured she wouldn't tell me if I was; I wondered if she even knew that she was. "You're zaftig." And I figured maybe that just meant fat in a different language and so I looked it up. *Curvaceous. Pleasingly plump.*

Boys liked me, my fleshy parts that made me different from the other girls. At the roller rink they'd ask me for couples skate, and sometimes even the moonlight skate when the lights went down and that mirror ball sent fireflies over the walls, the floors, our faces. And we'd circle the rink for a while, and the music was always slow. When I was really young, my mom brought me to the rink on

Saturday afternoons for kids skate, and there used to be an organ player, a real guy in a booth near the shoe rental, and he and my mom used to laugh together, and he'd play *I Dream of …* and he'd lean toward her and say her name then, and once I watched while she sat next to him on his bench, and he put his hand high on her leg while the other hand spread wide over a few chords. Now, though, it was records all together on a tape that hissed sometimes. And me and a boy would hold hands: palms wet and fingers laced, and he'd guide me off the floor and into a corner where during moonlight, kids would press up against the wall and make out until one of the guards, a high school boy with a whistle and a flashlight, would swoop in to break things up. But before that, one or another of my moonlight partners would put his tongue in my mouth and his hand under the buttons of my blouse and I knew then the foggy warmth of want. And I leaned into it, this want: the moist hands on my skin, the hot breath on my neck, the rub and hardness of him, of any him.

My mom, her daughter's mother, wanted to be loved. I could see it in her eyes when she'd come to me on those nights when she'd met someone. They were shiny and blinking, like she'd just seen something so bright it stunned her, and under her perfume and smoke and the greasy, fried smell she wore home from the diner was something else, a scent like honey and nuts. Her love smell, I called it. But not out loud. Just to myself. And on those nights of her love smell and blinking eyes she'd wake me up if I wasn't still there on the couch watching late night movies with Shanty on my knee, feeling her ribs through her fur. And her small hands would stroke and pat me while she told me about him. Any him.

"He's new in town," she'd say. Or "He's a business man." Or "He's smart." Ever hopeful, always optimistic. Once it was the insurance man who came into the diner after she'd gone to his office about grandpa's policy, the little pile of money in her name. He wore shiny, white shoes that looked like plastic and he had sandy hair that circled a pink bald spot on the top of his head. He called my mom Doll, up until the time he left because she wouldn't give him money to pay his rent. Another time, the man she met stole our car while she slept him off; and another time, a woman showed up at our door in the morning while the guy sat at our table drinking coffee and eating the runny yellow eggs my mother had made for him. He winked at me and told us he'd called his wife to come and pick him up.

And Mom would swear off guys for a little while then; but I never did, even when I started to hear things at school, small whispers behind my back in the halls, girls talking in the bathroom when they didn't know I was in there. You can guess the things they said, the names they called me, but that didn't matter. What mattered was the warmth that climbed and filled my insides in the dark corners of the roller rink, behind the bus garage at the edge of school property, in the back seats of cars we'd find with their doors unlocked at night. I'd come home breathless and sticky with sweat, grass in my hair, buttons undone, and the house would be empty (except for Shanty) until my mother came home from work, bored and lonely and ready to break her fast, eager to meet someone new. She liked her men skinny, like we used to be, like my father was, and they'd slide in and out of our life like a cat through a door barely opened.

It was my fault Shanty ran away. On a February night Mom called from the diner: "I've met someone. See you in the morning." It was just before my sixteenth birthday, so I didn't need her, I could take care of myself. And I went to the park where everyone hung out in the warm or the cold, and this night it was cold-cold, the kind of cold that makes your eyes water and your mascara freeze in clumps. The kind of cold you might wish you wore something other than a short skirt and tights and boots; you knew your legs would be blue from your thighs to your shins, and you couldn't keep your teeth from chattering or your hands from shaking. That kind of cold. The kind of cold when you paired up quick, found someone to warm your hands on, someone to huddle with against the wind. Like the guy you never saw before—I never saw before. Older and whiskers under his bottom lip in a shaggy patch, a scowl like nothing was any good at all. I saw him giving me an up and down and I saw how his eyes lingered on my tights, my pleasingly plump thighs, and on my coat stretched over my top parts. I asked him for a cigarette, even though I don't smoke, and lucky for me he didn't either. But he reached for me anyway, there in the shadow of the swing set, the monkey bars. He ran his hand over the arm of my coat, pinched through it to my flesh.

"This felt?" he asked. And before I could say I'd already heard that one, he said, "It is now." I laughed a little, it was so dumb but he was so cute, angles and planes, dark eyes and high cheekbones for a boy. He didn't laugh at all, though, and I thought he might turn away so before he could, I said, "Wanna come over?"

All the boys I knew, and I'd never asked anyone to my house before, because, frankly, part of the whole delicious deal was how it felt to be out somewhere, away from home and my mom and the men who didn't love her, like she deserved, like her father had—out in the dark corners or against a tree or stretched and twined in the grass. But it was cold, like I said, and why not?

I pulled his hand and he walked with me, a few steps back, but side-by-side sort of anyway, and that was new, too, my walking hand-in-hand with a boy over the ice-slippery sidewalks of my neighborhood where the streetlights and Christmas lights up too long made halos and colored pools in the snow. The windows of the houses were bright in the dark and there was a family sitting down to dinner; and there was a father in his recliner, sleeping it looked like, in the blue-gray TV light of the news, maybe; and there was a little girl up in her bedroom looking out at the sky. Her face pale and expectant, it looked like from my sidewalk point of view.

And Shanty ran out of the door when I opened it, even though the cold was too much for her I knew, fur coat or no, and I tried to reach down and scoop her up before she leapt from the step, but the boy—his name? Trevor, I think. Or Terrence—told me to let her go, he was allergic anyway, and he pressed me to the wall inside the door and kissed me with his teeth as much as his lips, his tongue, like I was something he wanted to chew on. He sunk his fingers into the soft flesh of my hips, making bruises I would find when I slid into my nightgown later. And he thrust against me, ground himself there, and all my cold parts went warm right away, and my mouth hurt but my body felt liquidy and golden, like honey in the sun. He pulled away long enough to scan the living room, the old television, the hook rug, the portrait of my mother my grandfather painted; and I could see he was a mean one, this one, his eyes were marbles and his face was tight. And outside on the stoop, Shanty meowed. Once, twice, then a yowl that followed us to the couch where Trevor-Terrence pushed me back on the butt-worn cushions and didn't stop although I said *no* once, a quiet little whisper that even I didn't believe, a token, maybe, what a girl should do. But this wasn't my first time so I knew what to expect, what I thought I wanted, and what he did, too. "You're a big one," the only thing he said during, and when he was done, he was gone. And so was Shanty.

I stood on the stoop in bare feet and legs, the concrete so cold it burned my soles. I tugged my skirt down over my blue, shaking thighs. The boy was a shimmer far down the street. "Shanty!" I called. "Shanty!" I cried.

And later, it sounded like cats fighting in my dreams, and I woke up to yelling, to howling, and to a car door slamming and tires on the icy pavement. I came to, blinking in the dark, listening before understanding that my mother had come home even though it was not yet morning, and she was downstairs, crying. I found her on the couch, still in her coat and scarf; her lip was bruised and bloodied.

"Mom," I said, and she looked at me and tried to smile.

"It's all right, Baby. It's fine." She stood and hung her coat on a hook near the door and I could see the scrapes on her knuckles. She saw me looking.

"Fucking men," she said.

And I said, "Yes." The insides of my thighs still hurt from the bony hips of Trevor-Terrence.

"I'm hungry," she said. And I said, "yes," again, because I thought that might be it, that might be what I was feeling, too, an ache and emptiness beneath my ribs. I went to the kitchen and made us cocoa and toast with strawberry jelly, and my mother ate four slices and dabbed at her broken lip with a paper napkin. Later, when I cleaned up, I saw the red on the white paper and didn't know what was strawberry and what was blood, and I tasted sour at the back of my throat. When we got up the next day it was almost noon and I made pancakes with butter and syrup and cinnamon.

As the winter passed we stayed in nights on the couch with the television going but the lights off and plates on our laps: spaghetti, beef stew, shepherd's pie, tuna casserole. Mom would go out just to smoke on the back patio, and I only went out to the front stoop and called, uselessly, for my cat.

When the man my mother had met, the one we'd been waiting for, finally showed up, it was nearly 1 a.m. and I was asleep with my head in Mom's lap. I felt it when she slid out from under me, holding me with her little hands and settling me easy on the cushions like something that might break. I pretended to be asleep and through my eyelashes in the flickering light of the TV I watched her go to the door, watched the man come in, dirt on his face and muddy to his knees. He hugged her tight and spoke into her hair and I could hear it: *stuck…tow truck…walked…so sorry*. He sounded like it all hurt him, and like holding her might help. He pulled back and kissed her lightly on the lips, on the neck, on the scars on her arms. He kissed her small hands, open like cups at his chin. The man glanced over her head and at me on the couch, and before I closed my eyes I could see he was fat like Mom, like me, maybe, and he had a soft, round face that looked—well—nice.

They went to her room and I could hear them through the wall. "I'm sorry," he said, and he said it again, "I'm so, so sorry. Your daughter. Our plans," he said. "Shhh," she said, and things rustled and creaked and I got up from the couch and on bare feet I went outside into the night. It was too late for the park, the cops kicked us out at curfew, but that wasn't where I wanted to be anyway; I hadn't been there in months. I walked a little, feeling the cement still holding its day-warmth under my bare feet. In my neighbors' windows there was nothing but dark, and my shadow under the streetlights looked big and round.

A few houses down a sprinkler—on a timer, I guess—hissed and spit and stutter-sprayed a garden, and a cat jumped out from under the bushes and ran. Shanty, I thought, because now, tonight, when my mother shared her bed with a fat, sorry, nice man, I thought maybe it could be; you never know.

The cat scrambled in my direction, leaping and running and swerving into the street close enough for me to see that it wasn't my cat, the one I lost, the one I missed. Still, I turned as it passed and watched it run, tail high and legs slightly out of line so it would look bigger. They do that, you know, make themselves bigger to ward off their predators. I watched as he hurtled through the night, wondering where he would go.

I stood on my street, a block from home. Where, I wondered—the ones who are lost—where do they all go?

Salvage

Daddy shopped salvage. Tins, those were his favorite. Unmarked cans, their labels stripped from their curved bodies. Dented, some of them. Those were the ones Mother feared most: Never, ever eat from a dented tin, she warned us. You boys hear me?

Saturday mornings, Daddy would pack me and my brother in the station wagon and drive to New Hope, two towns over. "Railroad Salvage" was the sign above the shop's door. A white plank with painted black words, a thing that looked like the stuff inside, battered and worn, the letters big and small, no pattern, no discernible sense of order. Mother preferred order. Daddy was a fan of mess and the surprises found in it.

Why railroad, I wondered, walking the narrow, winding paths through plastic sleeves of tube socks, snow shovels with broken handles, lampshades torn and yellowed, three-legged chairs, label-less tins. I imagined hobos, like those in the stories Daddy read to us over and over in his voice that sounded like music. Mellow, deep, like a bass guitar. Me and little Jakey under the blankets in our skinny bed, listening, listening. Hobos, I imagined, with packs made from bandanas and sticks slung over their shoulders, tossing cans off a moving caboose, hurling chairs and lampshades, socks, to their buddies (the salvage store proprietors) in the weeds along the tracks.

Like Daddy, I loved the cans most of all. Dinnertime when Mother was working, because—as she said—somebody had to, Daddy would strew a bunch over the counter, tall and squat, shiny and dull, dented and not. He'd sing then, that Danny Boy song, only Donny, he'd say. Me, my name. And one after another we would open things: canned meat, gray and smelling of pepper; olives, their red stuffing vibrant, soaking in murky oil; something like marshmallow fluff, only not, like frosting, but no. We'd pass the cans between us, Daddy, little Jakey, me, pushing our forks into them, chewing with our mouths open, smiling.

Once there were worms inside. Wiggling around finger-sized ears of corn. We threw that can away. Once, it was snakes. The springy kind made of cloth and coil, shooting up past my nose when I pried the can open. Little Jakey, atop a phone book on a chair at the kitchen table, laughed and laughed. I did, too, once the fright slowed in my chest. Daddy didn't notice, his face toward the window over the sink. Out, looking out.

Rubber balls. Plastic fangs. Miniature tubas. Glass eyes. More and more stuff. Less and less often food. It was fun at first, this daily dinnertime treasure hunt. Until we got hungry.

Mother worked until midnight. We could hear her, little Jakey and me, walk up the gravel drive, hear her come into the kitchen and gather the cans to throw in the trash. We could hear her put away the bread and cheese she'd brought home from the all-night shop where she worked in town, and we could hear our stomachs rumbling, our father snoring.

Once, after the salvage was ropes of plastic beads and cotton balls and condensed milk, I heard Mother in the kitchen, the familiar chuck and hiss of the can opener. I climbed over little Jakey and crept out of bed, my stomach rolling with nothing but the sweet thick of condensed milk.

There she was, Mother at the table, a hand under her chin. She turned the can upside down and I waited for the spill, boiled peanuts or brass rings or (how I would dream this moment later and always) teeny tiny men who looked like fathers or hobos, landing on their feet and scampering away like insects in a sudden light.

The can was empty.

Daddy was gone.

Twenty years later as I make chain-store-bought beans and franks for my own boy Jake, my wife at the breakfast bar laughs when I hold the can up to my ear before I open it. I shake it a little and listen some more. Donny, she says. Shh, I say to her, and she covers her mouth with her hand, but her shoulders shake and her eyes glimmer and I love her so much it makes my toes tingle. Shh, I say to my little Jakey, in his highchair and giggling and banging a spoon on his tray.

I listen harder, the cool of the can against my cheek. And there it is, quiet, in the tinny slosh and tumble of whatever is inside. The low and lonely whistle of a train passing in the night. Deep notes from a bass guitar.

My father's voice.

Things You Know
But Would Rather Not

She knew she was dying. No one could tell her anything different. When Mary Alice woke up in the morning she could feel it in her bones, in her heart, the slight ache and rattle, the slow chug that felt like an engine unwilling to start. She'd work to extricate herself from the pile of things that blanketed her during the night: her three cats, Jax, Jill, and Eddie; the books she'd been reading (*The Outsiders, Jane Eyre, Go Ask Alice, Algebra I, Symptoms and Early Warning Signs*); the wrappers from the Suzy Qs she'd bought at the hot dog stand on her way home from school and had stashed in her bedside table with the bags of chips, the Reese's she'd lifted from the 7-Eleven, for that moment when she would wake with a start in the deep dark and feel the ravaging hunger like teeth in her belly; the orange and green afghan her grandmother (dead before she was born) had made for her father (out of the picture before she was two except for his monthly checks in the mail); the mimeographed pages of her homework assignments that still smelled of glue; a scattering of pens and her journal where before she'd fallen asleep she had practiced writing swear words in first cursive, then thick block letters. Her favorite, she'd concluded, was shit.

Her mother was hardly ever up when Mary Alice got out of bed in the morning; didn't matter if it was a school day or like today, a Saturday. Mary Alice could hear the radio alarm going down the hall, a tinny whine of static and voices and the Saturday morning countdown that was never quite enough to push through the deep sleep of her mother, Sam. (Her name was Sally, really, but she liked to be called Sam, a man's name.) Mary Alice made her own bed, pulling the corners tight and tucking her pillow under the afghan; she built neat piles of books and papers on her bedside tables; she pet the cats and swept crumbs from the bed and up from the floor, and went to her mother's room to shake her awake. Then she would go make the coffee, the Tang and the toast, get the day started. These were no easy tasks for a girl who knew she was dying. And besides, she was only thirteen. Why did she have to do everything?

"Can you get me my ciggies, hon?" Sam asked before her eyes were fully open. Mary Alice breathed in the ashy smell of her mother's room, the stale smoke of it. It smelled, too, like the chemicals Sam used in her darkroom: gummy, sharp. And there was something else—Mary Alice tried to breathe through her mouth, to swallow the smell before it lodged in her nose, in her forehead—something sour and yeasty. A pair of socks that were far too big for her mother's tiny feet ("These puppies haven't grown a bit since I was twelve," she liked to brag when she and Mary Alice went shoe shopping, which they had to do every six months with Mary Alice's big and getting-bigger-all-the-time dogs) were stretched out on the plush white rug at Sam's bedside. They looked sinister there, Mary Alice thought, long and snake-like.

She went to the table under the window, the little round thing her mother kept covered with a velvet cloth that was marked now with cigarette burns and mug stains. Two packs of cigarettes were there, a red and white box and her mother's Camels. A glass with something brown and the doused butts of last night's smokes, another with lipstick on its edges. Sam pushed herself up in the bed, her shoulders knobby beneath the straps of her undershirt. Her hair fell to her biceps, her boobs jiggled. She had raccoon-y mascara circles under her eyes and she looked like a picture, but not just any old picture, she looked like a painting, like something in a museum. Sam looked— Mary Alice could never quite get over this—gorgeous. Her mother was gorgeous.

The smoke clouded in the space between them, and her mother inhaled hard, thirsty for it. Mary Alice thought it might be the smoke that was killing her. The way the house reeked of it, the way it filled her own lungs when Sam gulped at it like this. Yes, maybe it was the smoke.

Or perhaps it was that she simply could never get enough sleep. Mary Alice had read somewhere that teen-agers needed more sleep than adults do, maybe as much as babies even. They were still growing, their brains still forming. But there was too much noise, sometimes, and too much quiet other times, and Mary Alice would wake up in the middle of the night to the noise or the quiet, her bedside light—left on from her reading herself into sleep—shining like a headlight through her dreams. Mary Alice admired the way her cats were able to sleep all the time no matter the circumstances, getting up long enough to eat, maybe drink, jump to a windowsill to chitter at a bird in a nearby tree, then back to sleep in tight circles, or on hot days, long stretched-out things. Like these socks, the ones on her mother's rug.

Mary Alice kicked them under the bed.

"Late night?" she asked.

"Hmmm?" Sam said, distracted as always, plucking tobacco off her tongue with her manicured nails, sharp and purple. Didn't most people smoke cigarettes with filters these days?

If she squinted just right, the smoke and the shiny silvery sheets her mother slept on made things look not like a painting as Mary Alice had thought, but like one of those photographs Sam would take. Black and white and all sorts of shades of gray. Like the ones in the galleries. They looked dirty to Mary Alice, those photos. Dirty and beautiful. Except, of course, the ones of her.

Things she hated:

1. Having her picture taken.

2. Dogs.

3. School (not the classes, really, the learning part—but the other stuff. The kids, none of them her friends. The teachers. The low-slung building that too many students crammed into and so her grade, grade 7, had to go out back to the mobiles for class, those tin box trailers that dipped and sprung when you climbed up into them, that rattled when the winds came, when the spring rains started.)

4. The war. (She didn't know much about this one, but she was sure it was wrong. There were protests. Kids got shot at a college in Ohio because of it. Or something like that.)

5. Tang.

6. Her mother. (Not really.)

7. The way her boobs were starting to bounce when she walked. That she was going to need a bra soon.

8. Lists.

9. The creepy guy next door who was old but played basketball in the driveway after it got dark.

10. Being something that wasn't really a kid, but wasn't an adult, either.

You'd think Mary Alice would hate that she was dying, too, but she didn't. She liked it. It gave her something to focus on. Something all her own to look forward to.

Her mother kept on smoking and Mary Alice went to make the coffee, to prepare the Tang. To check the fridge for food she was pretty certain wasn't there except for butter maybe, or margarine. And grape jelly she liked to eat by the spoonful. She passed through the den with its soft leather furniture, its paneled walls, its red shag rug. Mary Alice tried not to look at the photos over the couch, the ones of her when she was little, pretty, blond and big-eyed, naked and sitting on the beach in one, on a tree stump in another. The one, too, of her crying, her face so red you could even tell in the black and white of the photo, a deep crimson-like gray. Her little arms wrapped around her chest, hugging herself—like if she let go, she'd fly away. And somewhere in the way back background, a station wagon with wood panels, a wooden fence, a tiny house. She didn't know where they were, the picture was years and years old, in the olden days it could've been, because she was wearing something weird, puffy and gauzy and scalloped with ribbons everywhere. Wherever they were, though, when this picture was taken, Mary Alice was pretty sure her dad was there, too.

But she didn't pay attention to those photos; they were a landscape she was so familiar with she didn't see it anymore. Like the sound of the heavy ticking of the grandfather clock on the bookcase also in the den, a sound that Mary Alice forgot about because it was always there. So when she actually heard it lifting out of the other sounds of the house (refrigerator hum, murmur of her mother's radio, tick of the baseboard heaters on cold mornings), it startled her.

"Jacques the croc, swallowed the clock," she said to the clock like she did every morning when it struck seven, eight. It had been her grandfather's, Mary Alice was pretty certain. Or perhaps her grandmother's—she thought maybe she believed it was her grandfather's because it was a grandfather clock. She could be like that, she knew. Literal. She didn't actually know her grandparents. None of them. They all died young, she suspected. She wasn't sure. It probably was like that in her family. Dying young.

Mary Alice started with the Tang, dumping tablespoons of the powder into a small pitcher. The dust of it flew into her nose and she sneezed; its sweetness coated her sinuses and made her gag. Later, her mother would pour two glasses and Mary Alice would drink hers down quick trying not to breathe, to smell it, to taste it. And Sam would pour a little something in her own, a pick-me-up she'd call it, a day-starter.

The refrigerator smelled like metal inside, cold and sharp. Jars of things rattled in the door: mustard, ketchup, horseradish, herring in cream sauce that was so old Mary Alice had never not seen it there. Boxes of film filled the crisper. Nothing edible. She could make a shopping list, but she didn't want to, she hated lists. Instead Mary Alice filled the coffee pot with water and scooped in the coffee, and it occurred to her that she was unable to swallow. *Dying,* she thought. *I'm dying.* And she tried and tried to swallow, the back of her tongue still tasting of Tang. She lifted her chin up, ducked her head, but it wouldn't work. Jax, the marmalade cat of her trio jumped up on the counter next to the range, pushed her head against Mary Alice's soft stomach. Cats always knew.

"Swallow," Mary Alice commanded herself, and Jax mewled, which gave Mary Alice the idea to rub her fingers up and down her own throat, like they did with the cats when they had to pill them. She rubbed and rubbed, and yes! To her great and frantic relief, Mary Alice swallowed. She gulped. She did it twice more just to show that she could—gulp, gulp. Loud swallows like a bad actress. Jax jumped off the counter.

To Do:
(This was why Mary Alice hated lists. Her mother was a list-maker. She had them all over the house, like this one here on the fridge held by a magnet that looked like a carrot. One of her usuals, the list of Saturday chores for Mary Alice.)
1. Laundry. (And this one had a sublist, in case Mary Alice might forget.)
    a. Collect
    b. Wash
    c. Fold
    d. Put Away
2. Cat litter.

3. Dusting.
4. Homework.
5. Change Sheets.
6. Pose.

Shit. Shit shit. It had been months since Mary Alice had to pose for her mother. Sam was onto something different for a while, taking her camera to the parking lot at Jack's Super, sitting there in her Volkswagen, smoking, watching. She had a show coming up soon, and she'd been shooting for days, developing deep into nights. She'd tried a few rolls of color film, too, making photos that Mary Alice saw hanging from the line in the darkroom next to the kitchen and off the garage. Bright things that looked like images out of the movies: shining cars and people talking, close-ups of cans of beans, watermelons, shopping carts, sales signs (done in a way you couldn't read the words, but could see a letter or two, or a curving line with the blur of a head or something passing in front of it).

Mary Alice loved these photos. Loved loved loved them. She loved, too, that when her mother took pictures in the grocery store like this, she actually bought things, and there would be food in the house, things to make into real meals. But then one night, while she sat up reading in bed with Jax on her lap and Jill (the tabby) and Eddie (the gray) at her ankles, Mary Alice heard her mother down in the darkroom, throwing things, yelling, crying. Then she heard noises in the kitchen, water running, ice trays cracking, cabinets slamming. And her mother muttering, talking like someone was there, but there wasn't, Mary Alice was pretty certain. Not this time. In the morning Mary Alice slept late and came to thickly, her engine slow but not yet dead, and the house smelled like bacon and Sam was already up and cooking, stirring the Tang, the kitchen sparkling clean around her, the door to her darkroom open, everything in place, nothing hanging on the line to dry. Later, when Mary Alice changed the litter box, she found the color photographs in shreds in the garbage can at the edge of the driveway.

Things she loved:
1. Her cats. (All cats, really. Cats. Cats were good.)
2. Shit. (The word. She really loved it.)
3. Sleep.
4. Her mother. (Mostly.)
5. Making things clean.
6. That life could not possibly be long. Life was short. Everyone said so. And wasn't this something to look forward to?

She poured the coffee for her mother, black and strong, and one for herself with Coffeemate and sugar, lots of it, and wiped the sticky drink powder from the counter, rinsed the dishrag, hung it over the neck of the faucet. Mary Alice carried the mugs back to her mother's room, where Sam had moved from the bed to the table by the window, list-making and smoking and studying contact sheets with a magnifier that looked like a shot glass. She patted her knee for Mary Alice to sit, which she did, but hated. (11. Sitting on her mother's knee.) Sam's legs were bony and hard, and Mary Alice was fat, she knew it, bigger than her mom, and she had to balance on her mother's knee while holding her weight off of her sort of, and she could feel her own legs, plump, white limbs that stuck out from under her nightgown, shake with the effort. Sam swept Mary Alice's hair to one side and said, "Know what the back of little girls' necks are for?" before she kissed her daughter's neck. It was swift and sweet, and something she'd done pretty much every morning for as long as Mary Alice could remember. She could feel her mother's breath warm on her skin; the kiss both embarrassed and delighted her.

"Not really a little girl anymore," Mary Alice said and stood up from her mother's knee. She pulled another chair close to the table and sat. She brushed ashes into her palm. Rubbed them away on the hem of her nightgown.

"You'll always be my little girl," Sam answered on cue. She was back at her writing now, making her list and reciting her part of the script like a poem they said by heart together, alternating lines.

"Even when I die?"

"Even when you die."

When had Mary Alice added that line, *even when I die*? She thought it must have been ages ago, she couldn't remember not saying it. Had she always known she was dying? Jax and Jill and Eddie were rolling over one another in the hallway just outside her mother's doorway. Jax landed on Jill's back and Eddie crashed into them. They made noises in their throats and hissed, just playing. Every now and then one or another of them would stop and lick a paw, turn away from his buddies, stare at Mary Alice at the table. They rarely came into Sam's room.

"Did you see the list?" Sam asked, her head still over the notepad in front of her. She was drawing little asterisks down the margin. Sometimes it was asterisks, stars, sometimes it was numbers. Today looked like a star day for lists.

"Umm hmm." Mary Alice swallowed the sugary, beige coffee, looked out the window but there was nothing to see. The basketball in the strip of grass between their driveway and the neighbor's. The street. The houses. All kind of like theirs, long and sleek with flat lawns and bushes shaped like walls and boulders. Ranch houses she knew they were called, but she didn't know why. They were miles away from horses, states away maybe.

"Let's get started, then," Sam said and stubbed out her cigarette. She sipped at her coffee and tucked the notepad into the waistband of the shorts she slept in. "The light is good, I think. We don't have a lot of time."

"We don't," Mary Alice agreed.

Her mother's last show was at a gallery in the city, in a neighborhood of high rises and small, expensive shops and restaurants. Mary Alice counted the number of men in uniforms and caps, standing just outside entrances, at the ready to pull open car doors and ring buzzers. Some had whistles. The doormen nodded at them while they passed, and Sam gave the men her asterisk smile, the one that glinted in her lipsticked mouth, that shined like something neon, or like a flash from her camera. Mary Alice, twelve then and in new purple velvet bellbottoms and a flowering silk blouse, trotted along at her mother's side, trying to match her walk that was both brisk and slinky. Like the cats, she thought, the way their bodies moved in long, curving lines when they hurried down the hall to the kitchen at dinnertime. Sam wore an ankle-length leather coat the color of cream, and a fuzzy golden tam. It was autumn and Mary Alice's mother was beautiful.

The gallery was already full of bodies and chatter when they arrived, its wide windows cloudy with warmth and breath. Men in jackets and turtleneck sweaters, women in long skirts or wide-legged pantsuits gathered in groups of three and four, smoking, lifting glasses, eating crackers topped with swirls of cheese and tiny pickles. Some huddled in the middle of the room glancing over their shoulders, while others moved along its edges, studying the photos, dozens and dozens of them like a gray border half-way up the stark white walls. They were small, and so you had to lean in close to get a good look.

How to behave at an opening when you are only twelve:
*Smile.
*Don't eat too many crackers with cheese.
*Say please and thank you.
*Come when your mother calls, but don't cling.
*Don't let people know you are eavesdropping even if they say things like: "That poor dear" or "what kind of mother" or "shh, she's right there."
*Don't look at your reflection in the glass frames over the pictures from when you were little and beautiful. Because you are neither of these things anymore.

It was here at the gallery on this opening night that Mary Alice figured she must be dying. She bent toward a photo of her legs in a pair of her mother's white patent boots in the doorway of the garage, the cats at her ankles. She liked this one. A man in a brown shining suit and a woman in a tin-colored blouse with silver beads that jingled as she lifted her glass stood close by in front of a different photograph. When they spoke, Mary Alice pretended not to hear.

"Is she ill?"
"Oh no, I don't think so."
"Her face looks so sad."
"Those eyes."

"Those pudgy little legs."

"Those big feet."

When they turned and saw her there they smiled, but more like grimaces than grins, and moved on to the next photo, the breeze of their escape lifting Mary Alice's bangs from her forehead. She felt hot, dizzy. She pressed the cool glass of club soda against her face. She stepped closer to the photo they'd been looking at, one her mother took on a recent morning before Mary Alice had gotten out of bed. Her hair was everywhere on the pillow; she was tangled in sheets and books and cats. You could see the bruises on her shins, the ones from the everyday use of her legs, her big feet. There was a shadow at the tops of her legs, just under the sheet, something black and mysterious. She looked closer. It was true what they said; her eyes were foggy, not right. Was she ill? She couldn't remember now. All she knew for certain was that she was hideous. People could see her like this. She wanted to die. She felt something rumbling inside her. She gulped soda and wanted more, needed more. She was thirsty like a cat in the desert. She was hot, so hot. She was—Mary Alice hoped, no, was sure—dying.

The Saturday morning shoot started out okay, fun even, with Sam in one of her high, good moods, running from place to place in the shopping center, working her light meter, swinging her camera on its leather strap around her neck. She laughed and Mary Alice laughed, too, because why not? There were so many other times to be sad, to be dying, she thought today she might try something else. Living, maybe. And why was that? The warm spring sun that shone on them as they drove in the Volkswagen with its top down, the way boys looked at her mother and then Mary Alice and nodded hello. She was beautiful in Sam's light, Mary Alice was pretty certain, in the clothes her mother had chosen for her from her own closet: a long camel-colored vest that swept in circles around her knees, a silk scarf with squares and rectangles of green, of orange, of pink. Flowing pants that were almost a skirt. And at Loehmann's, Sam bought Mary Alice a floppy hat, like something from an ad, that one on the billboards for women's cigarettes, maybe, or a Pepsi commercial. The brim dipped low over Mary Alice's eyes that her mother had made big with mascara, a bit of shadow. Sam was scrubbed clean and looked trim and efficient in cowboy boots and jeans, a turtleneck shell with no sleeves that showed the balls of muscles in her arms, the freckles on her shoulders. They stopped in front of a toy store, the sort of place Mary Alice had never shopped, she was never much for toys, and Sam asked her to bend forward and look at a train on a track, had her frown. Inside the store, Mary Alice gathered up armloads of Barbies and hugged them all to her chest—as Sam instructed—and looked up towards the ceiling. Sam clicked and laughed, clicked and laughed. People stopped and watched as the shoot went on. Some asked questions.

"Is this for a catalog?" From a woman with a sheer scarf tied under her chin and bobby pins holding curls near her ears. Mary Alice loved that she might be mistaken for a catalog model.

"What kind of camera is that?" A man in a windbreaker asked. He held a little girl's hand and a dog on a leash. He smiled at Sam. The nosy dog sniffed Mary Alice's knees.

"Are you famous?" The little girl asked. She wore a yellow tutu and a sparkling plastic tiara.

"Yes," Mary Alice said.

Late in the afternoon Mary Alice and Sam stopped for an Orange Nehi and a plate of French fries at the cafeteria in Woolworths. They sat in a booth surrounded by dozens of shoppers at rest. Mary Alice poured ketchup onto the plate with the fries, a pool for dipping. She ate one fry, then another. She was famished, starving. Hours had passed since she'd toasted the last heel of bread and spread it with margarine and grape jelly.

It smelled like tuna salad and hot grease at Woolworths, Mary Alice always thought so. And like wet wood chips, like sawdust. Close by were the cages of small animals and birds, she could see the pink noses of things from where she sat, and hear the tiny living sounds they made. She pushed the plate of fries toward her mother over the sticky table. Mary Alice wished she had remembered to bring her wet'n'dries so she could clean things up a little. Sam nibbled a fry and lit a cigarette. She read from her list.

Possible backdrops:

*Toy Store. ("Check," Mary Alice said, and sucked the orange drink through her straw, swallowed easily.)

*Travel Agency. ("Check," Mary Alice said even though they hadn't actually gone into the place, but instead she was instructed to look longingly in the window at the posters of Paris, of Yellowstone.)

*Hardware Store. ("Check," Mary Alice said. She loved the oily smell of that place, a smell that made her think of men, of fathers.)

*Housewares. (And here Sam shook her head and drew a line through the word.)

Mary Alice leaned forward to see the other places on the list, and the floppy brim of her hat knocked her mother's glass over on the table. Ice and soda splashed everywhere, soaking the fries and turning the ketchup into soup, filling the plastic ashtray and dousing the freshly-lit cigarette. An expanding river of orange ran toward her mother's camera.

"You little…!" Sam hissed, and grabbed the camera up and away from danger. A waterfall of orange spilled over the edge of the table onto Sam's bluejeaned knees. The glass hit the floor and shattered.

"Shit!" Mary Alice whispered, something she'd never said before in the company of another person, and quick as that her mother slapped her across the mouth—something she'd never done before. Ever.

At the tables close by, people stopped their conversations and stared at the mother and daughter. Mary Alice felt her eyes burn and fill. She felt her chest seize. She tried to swallow, but couldn't. Tears leaked down her cheeks. She needed to swallow. She slid out from the booth, banging her shin on the table leg on the way.

"Oh damn, hon. Oh damn. Bad me. Bad Momma." And Sam reached toward her daughter, but Mary Alice spun and walked away. She wanted to run, but people already were watching, and what was the huge drama anyway? A girl fighting with her mother. No big deal. Look away now, look away. Mary Alice pulled the brim of the hat further over her face and tried desperately to swallow while she navigated the maze of aisles between tables and booths and animals in their cages and hurried toward the bathroom.

Her blouse was spattered with Orange Nehi and ketchup, and of course that would not do. Mary Alice made sure the bathroom was empty and pulled off the vest, unwound the scarf, unbuttoned the blouse. Goosebumps. Her boobs were low pink hills over the naked roundness of her belly that bounced as she swallowed, finally, swallowed and swallowed air, gulping down the crying that was right there in her eyes, in her chest, in her throat. She could see it all in the mirror. She turned the water to cold—cold was best for food stains, she knew—and held the blouse under the tap. Behind her, the door opened and in the mirror Mary Alice could see her mother standing there, camera around her neck, the knees of her jeans dark and wet-looking.

"Oh, honey," she said. Mary Alice thought her mother looked really sad, really sorry, and if she didn't have to get her blouse cleaned right in that instant, Mary Alice might even have gone to her, hugged her, forgiven her. Her hands went red and cold under the sink's spray. She swallowed because she could; she dipped her head and the brim of the hat fell over her forehead. Mary Alice studied the disappearing orange stain under water.

When she looked up again, the stain was pretty much gone, but her mother wasn't. There stood Sam, camera to her eye, the lens focused on Mary Alice in the mirror.

They took a long way home, detouring through the city where Sam parked the Volkswagen in front of a fire hydrant and asked one of the uniformed doormen to watch the car, to watch Mary Alice while she popped for just a second into the gallery. Mary Alice stared at the sun (you weren't supposed to do this, you could go blind) as it sank over the tops of the buildings. She blinked and saw stars in her eyelids, and saw shadows in the sky. Her blouse was wet under her mother's vest; she was cold and hungry and wanted the doorman to stop watching her. It was ages before her mother returned, excited and chatty. Mary Alice pretended to listen but didn't, instead, she played with the hamster her mother had bought her at Woolworths after she'd shot a roll of film in the bathroom. She tickled its nose through the skinny bars of its cage. She felt the pins of its little teeth on the tip of her pinky.

It was full dark when they pulled up to the house and the old guy was out dribbling the ball in his driveway. He waved at Sam and Mary Alice, and Sam waved back. Mary Alice carried the hamster to her room; Jax and Jill and Eddie followed her, howling and hungry and onto the scent from the cage.

Things You Know But Would Rather Not:

1. That the only food in the house is for pets, not people.

2. That when your mother closes the darkroom door behind her, you are on your own.

3. That care and feeding is up to you. And that you are still only thirteen.

4. That creamed herring does go bad, no matter what your mother told you. And that Tang can be eaten for a meal if necessary, straight out of the jar by the spoonful, swallowed down until you can't swallow anymore. And then you won't be hungry.

5. What the top of your mother's head looks like in the dark when you watch her from your bedroom window cross the grassy patch between your house and the neighbor's and he drops his basketball and puts his hands on your mother, on her butt, under her shell.

6. That you should not let a hamster out of its cage when there are cats in your bedroom.

7. That your mother loves you best when you are ugly.

8. What dying sounds like. And that cats don't like the taste of spleen.

9. That when you wake in the dark to another sound, someone yelling, crying maybe, but moaning you figure—Jesus. God. Jesus God—you think it could be your own dying finally. But there you are, under the blankets with the cats in circles at your ankles and on the pillow. And you hear it again, from the room down the hall: Jesus. God. And still, damnit, you are alive.

10. Shit. You are alive.

Good News Or Money

Hello. Is this someone with good news or money? No? Goodbye.

Er…

Hello. Is this someone with good news or money? No? Goodbye.

Ha! Yeah, right. *A Thousand Clowns.* Jason Robards. Right. Okay, yeah. Hey. It's me. Surprise. Long time. I know. So here's the thing. It's about Mom. Are you there? Are you listening? Can you hear me? It's about Mom; she asked me to call. I didn't want to, but she asked.

Hello. Is this someone with good news or money? No? Goodbye.

Goddamn machine. You wait a minute to try to collect your thoughts. It's about Mom, right? I got something to say. Goddamn machine. Who uses a machine anymore anyway? What is this, the 1980s? It's about Mom. Oh wait. You probably think I'm calling about something bad. Oh, jeez. Wow. That's not—I mean—it's not bad. Nothing bad. No, hey. It's good. Okay, take two. Or whatever.

Hello. Is this someone with good news or money? No? Goodbye.

Hi, Dad? It's me. You know. Your daughter? The one you haven't seen in what, six, seven years? Not since you moved up north. To the tundra or whatever. Well, the only one, I guess. Your only daughter. Maybe. As far as I know. Probably. Your only daughter, probably. Does that sound harsh? Sorry. It's just . . . I've been thinking about things, you know? Things. Just things. All kinds of things.

Hello. Is this someone with good news or money? No? Goodbye.

Goddamnit! Are you sure you aren't there? Pick up the goddamn phone, old man. You always loved that movie. *A Thousand Clowns.* I remember. You made me watch it with you, what, a hundred times? Jason fucking Robards. That little kid who looked like a miniature man. Anyway. Mom wanted me to call you. She's got some news. So yeah, good news, I guess. Good news. But no money. Ha! That's a laugh, me telling you no money. When was the last time you sent us any money, Dad? Daddy-o? Remember when I used to call you that? I was little. Really little. Daddy's Little Girl you used to call me. I'm seventeen now. But you know that. You should. You do, don't you? I'm seventeen. Aw, shit. Hang on. I gotta blow my nose.

Hello. Is this someone with good news or money? No? Goodbye.

I keep expecting you're gonna pick up the phone one of these times. Maybe you do. Maybe you do pick up the phone. Funny, but when I remember your voice, it sounds like Jason Robards in that movie. Sorta smoked rough. Is that you, Dad? Are you on the line? So here's the thing, Dad. Daddy-o. I have been thinking about that one time for some reason. Remember? That time you came home without your shoes and said you'd given them to some guy on the street. Some guy who needed them more than you, some homeless guy who lived on the street you said (what street was that exactly, Dad? Daddy-o. I always wondered what street was that exactly). I'm a little off topic here. Mom asked me to call. That's why I'm calling. She asked me to. To tell you the news. But that time you came home without your shoes, Dad. I can't stop thinking about it. There you were, in socks on the icy tile floor of the foyer, and you said you gave this guy your shoes because it was cold and he was barefoot. It was early morning. Spring. I remember the sky was sort of purple, it was so early. Purple like a bruise. Like grape jelly. You remember. You must. We were in that yellow house in New Hope. The one with the tile floors and the toilet that always overflowed. The one with the basement that flooded all the time and smelled like wet dog. The one where Mom was pregnant for a little while. And then she wasn't. You remember. And we didn't know where you'd been, me and Mom, and then there you were, wiggling your keys in the door like you didn't know which one worked and then you were inside and we were watching TV, me and Mom, the morning news, just in case. In case you were on it. In case you were news. An accident or something. Hurt maybe. But you didn't look hurt. Just shoeless. And Mom was eating dry toast to try to keep from puking, the morning sickness was bad. And I was eating Lucky Charms. The yellow house. You remember.

Hello. Is this someone with good news or money? No? Goodbye.

Goddamnit! That was my fault that time. I hit the wrong button. So Mom's news. Yeah. But wait, the yellow house first. You went to bed without telling us where you were all night, but we could tell you'd been drinking (not like we didn't know that already, but we could tell). And Mom seemed okay that you had given your shoes away, happy even. Because it was something good you'd been up to.

She was like that for a long time, you remember. Always wanting things to be good, to be right. Even that time we—me and her, you were gone by then—got evicted and they threw all of our stuff out on the lawn, she was out there making neat piles in front of the yellow house, loading what she could into the taxi, but making sure the rest was all orderly. Right. It was better that way, she told me. Maybe. Whatever. But then a little later—I'm back to the morning you came home without your shoes. Sorry. Jumping around a bit here. Anyway, later that day without your shoes, when the sun was high and hot, and the kids were playing out in the backyards and someone was mowing the lawn somewhere—I always loved that smell of cut grass, so I didn't even mind when you made me do the mowing—this lady sneaks up our walk and takes something out from a shopping bag and she's looking nervous. And something else. Drunk, maybe. We're watching her out the picture window, me and Mom, we could see her from where we were on the couch. Do you remember that couch? You bought it on time. I came home one day from school, and it wasn't there anymore. Just a place on the rug that looked cleaner than the rest of the floor. So this woman is on the front step and Mom pulls open the door, and the lady is there stuffing something—notebook paper or something—into your shoes. Pushing the toes right up against the screen door, neat, like she's setting them out for you or something. And Mom says, "hey!" That's all she says: "hey!" The lady's eyes are sore-looking and blue and she smiles, says, "excuse me," says, "his shoes." And I'm over Mom's shoulder and the woman sees me and smiles again, but the smile breaks. Like it was plastic. Jeez, I don't even know what that means, but I thought that then. I remember it now. Her smile broke like something plastic. And she turns and runs away.

Hello. Is this someone with good news or money? No? Goodbye.

Okay. This isn't why I called. This trip down memory lane or whatever. I called because Mom asked me to. She wanted you to know. She's getting married. She's happy. She wanted you to know. But now I got something to say. I only now thought of it. And it's about your favorite movie. *A Thousand Clowns.* Jason Robards is a bad father. He's an asshole. In the movie, I mean. I never liked that movie. It made my stomach hurt. Because I can't help remembering the one time you sat there in the living room on a kitchen chair where the couch used to be with a beer beside you on the floor. And the damn tape of that movie is on and you are staring at it like it's something important, maybe. Like there is something you have to learn from it. "Dad," I said. "Daddy-o." Remember? And you didn't even look at me. "Mom's sick, Dad." And she was. She'd been bleeding all morning, only I didn't know that right then. I was too little to know much, but I knew enough. I knew she was curled up in a ball on the bed, and there was a towel underneath her and another one soaking pink in the bathtub. And she was sweating and crying. "She's sick, Dad." And you turned to me finally, and your eyes were big black holes. You blinked. And your face was wet. And you nodded. You got up then, and went into the kitchen. And I could hear you in there on the phone. And then you came back with a fresh beer and sat on the kitchen chair and rewound the damn movie to where it was before you got up. And in a few minutes I could hear a siren. So there's that. Anyway. Mom told me to call you. She told me to tell you she forgives you now, but I told her I wouldn't tell you that. Because really, who can forgive a father for loving a movie more than his own wife, his own daughter. Because I think that sums it up pretty goddamn accurately. And besides that, who can forgive a father for coming home without his shoes? Not me. No sir. Not me. Okay, then. That's all I got. No good news, not really. And no money. Just this. That's all. Okay. Okay.

Tommy On the Roof

In the dream he is flying. Moonglow on his face.

We used to climb out on the roof when we were kids. Nighttime, under the stars. Big sister (me) and little brother. He was scared at first, so small and blond. Afraid of heights, afraid of falling. When did that change? I held Tommy's hand as he stepped out of his window, kept him steady on his feet until he got used to looking down. The evergreen that Dad planted spread its needled arms over the gutter, reached for us. You couldn't see us from the street, thanks to that big, beautiful tree. You couldn't see anything. We were ten, twelve. Two years between us.

"High," he said, always a little man of few words, and I could hear it in his voice, the change that was coming, a squawk in the word's middle. "Like flying," he said. And Tommy let go of my hand, settled down on the blanket I'd brought out. I sat next to him and our knees touched. Dad was dead just two days then. Mom was drinking downstairs in the kitchen; we could see the light from the window beneath us, evergreen shadows thrown over the lawn. Sometimes we heard her wail. Folks say it's hereditary this thing, this thing that makes us feel empty, needy, yearning toward whatever fills us up. Dad was a junkie. Mom was a drunk. (She's not now, not anymore, she's

God-filled instead and I can barely stand to listen to her talk anymore, to her prayers of nothingness: "let go and let God." Let him what?) I liked boys. And he did, too, Tommy, my brother. And junk. And drink. Even as a kid. He was never big on God, though.

On weekend nights for months, years, we met up there, on the roof outside his window. Sometimes he'd be there first, sometimes I would. A bottle of something. Something to smoke. My window was at the back of the house and I would have to climb up the slant to the peak (split-level, same up and down the block only ours full of junkies and drunks even though you might not know it to look at us: station wagon, newspaper route, Mom at the bank and Dad gone so me pushing the lawnmower on summer days), and when I got up there I would look out on the dark world beneath me, the places I knew and didn't, over the rooftops of our neighbors, past the park and the trees, to the horizon. Then I'd whistle soft and Tommy would turn and tilt and there I was, his sister, towering over him, my head in the stars. I'd pretend to slip then, trip on a shingle, lose my footing, wave my arms, whisper "oh shit." And no matter how many times I did it, old joke, bad, old joke, my brother would freeze and draw breath loud enough to hear inside the house, probably. If anyone was listening.

One time I came over the peak and found him under the blanket we left up there always, days and nights, rain or clear—only him with Randy from down the street, a dark-haired boy from my grade, one I always wanted but could never have (even though I tried, tight jeans and flirting, tops you could see my nipples through), and they didn't notice me because they were looking at each other, heads together, blond Tommy, dark Randy, bodies pressed and moving, urgent. We stopped talking then for a while. Not because it was *a* boy up there with Tommy, but because it was *that* boy up there with Tommy. And he knew it, knew Randy was what I wanted. And it wouldn't be until later, much later when I read his diary as I packed up his stuff, sorted out what to keep and what to give away, that I'd find out Randy was there that night because Tommy had invited him. For me. For me.

It was Randy who was to blame, I wanted to believe. Because Randy was going steady. Promised to a girl with that stupid promise ring (a band, a diamond chip) and then he stopped talking to Tommy even though he made sure to talk about him. "Faggot." Not like we didn't know. Not like anyone didn't know. But still, Tommy was emptier than ever and used whatever he could to fill himself up, more so than ever, scary so, from right about then on.

And that's when I tried to talk to him again, but it was too late. He even said that: "Too late, sister. Too late."

The evergreen tree grew close to the house and its roots got into the foundation and Mom, sobered up and God-filled by then, got someone from the church to come. And I heard Tommy crying and watched the church man come out of my brother's bedroom before he cut down the tree, before he hauled it away. And you could see everything then. The street, the roof, the gutters clogged with needles, the blanket flattened on the shingles, the clouds' reflection skittering across Tommy's dark window.

When it came time for me to leave for college, Mom was proud and Tommy was in the basement then, moved with his stuff and his stereo and he kept his door locked and his music loud and he could sneak out from underground by the cellar door. And the day before I was meant to go,

Tommy was gone. Gone for good, I hoped. Not because I wanted him gone always, but because it was good I wanted for him, and I thought gone, gone from here, maybe he'd find good.

"Flew," the note on his pillow said.

Years later, he's there in my dreams, flying still. And now when I pull into the driveway of Mom's house, walk past the flimsy white plastic cross she has planted where the evergreen used to be, I can't help but look up to the roof, to Tommy's window. He's not there, he's never there. Good. Good and gone.

Still, I can't help but look.

What Girls Want

"What do girls want?" Gregory asked me. I could barely hear him; he was down on the garage floor, kneeling on an old, dried up oil stain and tickling the ears of Scout, his new puppy. His mom sent him over here; tired, I guess, of his questions, his neediness. Sometimes you could hear him in the backyard when she was out there sunbathing, circling her on the towel. "Mom, what does an eclipse look like?" "Mom, what kind of mileage does your car get?" "Mom, when can we get a dog?" And she'd wave him away sometimes, like a fly or smoke; other times she'd grab his wrist and pull him down to the ground next to her and whisper into his hair. So maybe she was tired of that. Or maybe she thought he should have some man-company. She being single and all.

"Excuse me?" I said. I pulled another bag of ice out of the freezer chest, put it in the wheelbarrow. I could hear the rest of the neighborhood outside, kids and cars and dogs. A lawnmower.

What can I tell you about Gregory? That he was smart. Quiet (except when it came to things he believed in, things he would get excited about, dogs, space, global warming, things that made his voice go reedy and loud and a little hard on the ears, sort of a like a clarinet played wrong). He was kind, mostly, and sensitive.

"Girls," he said, and looked up at me. His glasses were crooked on his face. His pupils were round and dark holes in the middle of blue-gray. "What do they want?"

"You talking about someone we know?" I crossed my arms over my chest, tried to swell up some and look—I don't know—protective.

Gregory didn't say anything for a long time. But when he did, it was quiet: "No. Maybe. No." And that's when his mom poked her head in the door at the side of the garage. She saw us there and pushed her hair back from her face, lifted her chin. Smiled at me.

"C'mon, G," she said. "Time for your meds."

You'd know Gregory if you saw him. Skinny back then, a slice of a boy, and short, a full head shorter than most of the kids in his class. Glasses. Clark Kent-y ones. Magnifiers that made his eyes look like fly eyes, round and bulging. He wore jeans and T-shirts with sayings on them, things about tree huggers, women and bicycles; I liked the *Star Trek* ones. Beam me up. You know.

When I saw him the other day, on the train and in that funny long wool coat with the flaps on the shoulders, I recognized him despite the beard, the hair, the way he'd grown up tall and sort of fat. And I couldn't help but remember little Gregory, who he used to be, and dressed in a black T-shirt with the picture of a monkey in a camo hat and the words "Viva la Evolution!" on it. I liked that one, too.

He was Melanie's best friend. And that is something I can't quite explain, but now, looking back, I guess it said something about her. That she was nicer than most other kids maybe, that she was definitely nicer than me, her stepdad. Because back then, much as I want to believe I liked Gregory, there was something about that way he looked at you when he thought you weren't being fair, wet-eyed and with his mouth open just a little bit, like he couldn't breathe any other way, and that something raked at me inside, and made me not like him, too.

Melanie, though, she was gorgeous then. Now, too, probably. Like her mother. Long dark hair that fell in waves, white skin that went pink in the sun, big hazel eyes. Twelve, they were twelve, Melanie and Gregory when this thing happened. Sixth grade. They'd known each other forever by that time, since they were toddlers in the mud puddles of our back yards.

Gregory and his mom, Sascha, lived behind me and Melanie and her mom, Dee, Dolores, in the new subdivision out by the highway where it used to be all farms and quiet roads. And our houses looked all just alike pretty much, even though there were six different plans, different colors on our shutters and doors and rooftops, different porches and decks. August Orchard they called the place, even though the trees—probably planted sometime in the last century—had been more or less clear cut. Just three of them were left: the one at the gate, the one at the water feature (a dug-out pond with a fountain thing in its middle), and the one in the front yard of the model home. Two of them were a little sick-looking and bare, but the one at the model was big and blooming. The landskeepers had to sweep away the apples from under it each fall to keep the bees and the rotten smell from getting too bad.

But when it blossomed, well, it looked like something out of an ad for mortgages or breakfast cereal or something.

The rest of us, the brand new homeowners back then, had no trees and not even a lot of grass at first, just these dirt lots where we planted and planted, flowers and bushes and tomatoes, hoping that something would take root, something would grow up good and strong like we wanted our lives to be in this pretty little muddy place. Like the pictures in the brochures with kids on bicycles and "active" grandparents stopping to tie their gym shoes at one of the benches near the pond and families carrying paper bags of groceries sprouting the green tops of carrots and bouquets of flowers.

More than ten years ago now.

I'm trying to think how things went back then. That one day in particular all those years ago, but the lead up to it, too, and the days after. And now I'm wondering when I'd stopped thinking about it, like I wondered that day when I saw Gregory on the train and he looked right at me, and that weird, bright fog in his eyes sort of burned away and he smiled, he knew me, I guess, best as he might know anyone these days. He smiled. And he stopped rocking for a minute. That's what he was doing on the train in that seat all by himself even though it was rush hour and the train was nuts to butts and there was an open spot next to him. But his rocking and humming and weird smell like burnt cat litter or something that came off that wool coat of his (did I say yet that it was hot outside? October but in the eighties and the sun low like it gets in autumn and coming in through the windows of the train like light through a magnifying glass) well, everyone pretty much gave him his space.

"Gregory," I said. I was about two bodies away from him, but I knew he saw me. And something lifted in me, like I'd swallowed something heavy and thick only I didn't realize it. Like that something had been inside of me for so long that I didn't even notice it until it was lifted like it was when I saw him, when I named him.

And he kept looking at me. Smiling, maybe, his lips pulled back, his teeth showing. And he nodded.

We'd been a family back then, but just a few years old, our family. Me and Dee and Melanie. And I suppose I was drinking back then, too. Not suppose. I was. I wasn't at first, but then I was. But still, Dee found something to love in me, lucky me, because she married me just a few months after we met in line at the post office in the city, her behind me and carrying a big box that she kept nudging into my back. And I didn't know it was her back there, I only knew that it was annoying, this corner digging in between my shoulders every few minutes. And right then I was sober, a few days at least, just into what would be one of my long stretches on the wagon—because of Dee, truth be told, and because of Melanie—and like always when I'd quit I was jumpy and angry and it was like everything hurt, even my teeth and my skin.

"Excuse me," I must've said back then, that day in the post office. "Do you want something?" I said. But when I turned around—all tight, twisted rubber bands and hot razorblades under my clothes and behind my eyes and in my chest, it felt like—I wasn't expecting Dee. We were eye to eye, and that's saying something because I am a tall man, long in the legs and the waist, heads over most people. And so was she. That phrase—a long, cool drink of water?—well they could have made that up for Dee, I'm telling you. That's what she was, like something cool and wet, and just looking at her calmed me, put a bit of the fire out.

She blinked. Those hazel eyes of hers had bits of gold in them, and her nose was sunburned and her hair was pulled back but loose a little behind her ears. And I was never one for love at first sight because, really, how ridiculous is that concept, loving something without knowing it. Some-one. But she looked at me like she knew me, and I swear I thought I knew her. But we didn't know one another. At least not yet. We asked each other: "Do you go to…?" And "Have you ever been…" And even "Where did you grow up?" But there was nothing between us before this moment, this very moment when it felt to me like there was everything between us and—if I had my way—there always would be. She'd put the box down on the floor when we started talking and she kicked it a little over the tiles as we inched forward in line, pushing at it with the toe of her white sneakers. Really, that was so cute.

And that's how things started. You can figure out the rest after that. Coffee, lunch, dinner, movies, her place, my place. Our place. Melanie, when I met her, she was like a bonus. She was four then, when Dee and I got together. And pretty as a doll, and sweet, like you couldn't believe. The two of them together, well, they were more than I knew I deserved.

We bought the place in August Orchard and started setting up a life, the three of us. And I was sober then, still, in the beginning and for a good long time, working and being a husband, a father, and nothing special. But really, it was all so special that it made me ache inside sometimes. And now and again at night I'd wake up in the dark and sure I'd heard—what? And I'd lie there, still as stone, something gathering under my sternum, and I'd listen. Listen. But aside from the crickets and peepers and the trucks on the highway a mile away, there was nothing.

Does it matter when I started drinking again? Does it matter how or why? Maybe, maybe not. But life seemed to speed up in those years and all of a sudden I was nearing forty and so was my wife, and my stepdaughter was almost a teenager and on that day, that day when Gregory and I had been in the garage and his mom smiled at me, we were all out back having a barbeque. Because that's what we did. That's what everybody did in that place where we lived; we had cookouts and block parties and fundraisers for our schools and garden walks now that things had grown; and we saw the same people all the time, and we told the same stories, and we lived the same damn lives. Each of us, I mean. Really. Like you could pick me up and put me in a different house down the street, one with a little screen porch like mine and a garage with a workshop, only a front door that is painted Adobe Sands instead of Tahoe Red and a bay window instead of a picture window looking out from the living room. And in that house that was mine, almost, I could be someone else's dad, someone else's husband, and it wouldn't matter. My life would be exactly the same.

At least, that's how it was starting to feel.

I'd already been drinking again by then, that day, I mean; you probably figured that out.

And the sun, on that day of the barbeque, was high and hot. And the sky was big and blue, with nothing to stop it, nothing to contain it. And that got me, you know? The feeling that things would go on and on, like that sky. There were dads at the grills and moms at the tables and kids running circles in the grass. I went inside the cold of my air-conditioned house, and pulled open the refrigerator, more cold air, but closed it empty-handed because I didn't know what I wanted. Outside again I spotted Dee talking to the old couple from down the way, and she was in a short denim skirt, something she'd had forever, since I first met her and had carried the memory of the pink, freckled skin of her legs around with me to the office, to the car wash, to meetings at the community center (back when I used to still go to them). And I still had that memory now, only that's all it was, a memory, because, like I said, she was nearing forty and things were different: thicker, saggier. She probably shouldn't be wearing a miniskirt like she did when she was in her twenties, and it irked me a little to see her like that, different now, less than perfect.

It irked me too, to see Melanie that day in her little two-piece, her legs growing like her mom's, her little boobs just starting to lift from the long flat plains of her body. Because she was beautiful, damnit, and growing up, and could have anything she might want—any friends, any boy, any future. Maybe even some kind of future that wasn't cookouts and gardens and block parties, but gatherings in tall buildings with expansive views over cities, lakes, oceans. Our own city wasn't far away, just a few miles on the train, but it might as well have been another world, the way we all had snuggled into this little, grassy life in our matching houses.

Melanie and Gregory sat on a blanket down near where his yard and ours grew into one another. Gregory's puppy

Scout was beside them, making yapping noises that were spikes in the air. Then he'd snap at the bees that floated by and run in crazy puppy circles and out in front of the house, into the lane, and back again. I watched them from the glider (we bought it the first summer we lived here, and it squeaked a little now, rusty and old) where I sat next to my cooler of beer. They were very intent on something: Gregory talking and talking, pointing, and gesturing, like he was drawing maps in the sky, in the grass. And he had these dark plastic clip-ons over his glasses, like some old guy, and a too-big fishing hat that flopped over his ears and the back of his neck. And that monkey shirt, and shorts. And brown socks. Funny I remember that now, the brown socks, but I do. And when I see Gregory on the train years later, I look at his feet and he has on shining new oxfords the color of black coffee and I can see his ankles, scraped and raw from the new, stiff shoes, probably, and no socks.

I'm taking a long time to get to things here. I know.

"What do you suppose they have to say to each other still?" And it's Sascha, Gregory's mother, and she sits on the glider next to me and it squeals under her weight, which can't be much. She's small, like her son, and cute still, even near forty herself. Bottle blond and tan—well, a little orange, really—but bouncy like a cheerleader always, and packed nicely into a sundress with straps over her shoulders and a skirt that swung around her knees. I looked from her—and she's smiling at me again—to Gregory, and I thought, not for the first time, how she didn't seem like she could be the real mother of this strange kid. She must've been homecoming queen, or in the court, at least.

"It's a plot, I think. To overthrow the world. Or maybe just August Orchard." And she laughs and it's a nice sound, a little husky (she's a smoker) and a little like a chime or something.

You see how this is going. Do I need to tell you the whole of it? In the meetings I used to go to, they would have us tell everything to everyone, make amends, they said. Only now I can't see the good in that. Sometimes people just really don't want to know. "Stop," Dee told me when I called to make amends a couple years later. "I don't want to know." "But," I said, stumped, because I was following the steps, following directions. "You will not make yourself feel better by making me feel worse," she said. "Keep it to yourself," she said. "I don't want to know." And she hung up the phone. And when I thought about it later, for weeks after, months, really, I could see her point.

So I'll skip ahead.

Me and Sascha volunteered for the beer and soda run, and I shouldn't have been driving, but she was drunk, too. And I was the man, and it was my car, so I slid in behind the wheel. And the hardest part was getting out of the driveway. Bikes and toys and the garden hose and stuff like a gauntlet, a steeplechase, and we stopped and started and swerved and braked, missing things mostly, but feeling the bump of what we didn't. The CD player's on loud enough to cover the sounds of the kids playing behind the houses, Gregory and Melanie calling "Scout! Scout!" And we're laughing and Sascha's grabbing the little pull-down handle over her door to steady herself, to hang on.

Things went fine to Jack's Supermarket, close as it was. Just out of the subdivision and up the road to the intersection and the new stop light. The parking lot was soft under our feet, that's how hot it was, and the air smelled like fried meat and spoiled fruit and charcoal starter, and the frozen air of the market made my skin go gooseflesh and my nose run. We grabbed a cart and pushed it up and down the aisles like we didn't know where anything was, like we were newcomers or newlyweds shopping for the first time, all four hands on the cart, hips bumping, sandals slapping the floor, giggling. Goddamn giggling.

We bought enough for a month of parties. And loaded it into the way back of the station wagon and got into the front seat and drove around behind the loading bays of the store and near the dumpsters and popped a couple of beers and started making out. I couldn't tell you then who started it, and I can't tell you now either, but we both went at it like we'd been waiting a long time, and maybe we had been, "Is this what you want?" I said or she did, and my hands were under her dress and she was pulling at my fly and we were like kids, banging knees on the steering wheel, smacking into the rearview mirror, laughing and gasping when I grabbed the right lever and the front seat—finally—reclined.

It didn't take long. And it wasn't her name I called out. Habit, I guess.

And right away, I knew I had screwed royally up.

"I'm pretty drunk," I said, tucking things back into place. I couldn't look at her.

"Fuck you," Sascha said. And before I could say anything else, she was out of the car and pulling her dress into place and running across the road back toward our homes.

I knew I should try to catch her, coax her back into the car, get our stories straight, but she was fast. And it took me a long time to get going I was shaking so bad, and I couldn't see for the crying.

The driveway when I got back was empty of its stuff. No bikes. No toys. And Dee was out there running the hose over the concrete, and rubbing her nose, pressing her palms into her eyes. She didn't even look up when I slid the car in next to the curb, under the branches of the willow we'd planted that first year, and I knew she knew.

When I got out of the car, I hitched up my jeans and felt that odd sensation guys feel after sex, a sort of dullness in their balls, and an emptiness in their bellies. And Melanie was in the picture window, looking out from the air-conditioned living room. She had on one of my T-shirts over her little swimsuit, a gray thing that went down to her knees, and her face looked purple in the shadow and light. And off somewhere, somewhere behind the house, the sounds of the barbeque were gone but there was a howling going on. What do they call it when an animal is hurt? Keening. That's it. Keening from the house behind our own. From Sascha's. From Gregory's.

"What?" I said when I got close to Dee and she let the hose drop and looked—not at me, but over me, over my head.

"You really don't know?" She asked the branches of the willow tree.

And that can be one of those trick questions. Like cops when they pull you over: "Do you know why we pulled you over, sir?" "Yes, officer, because you could see the marijuana bulging out of the trunk of my car."

"Know what," I said. Because really, maybe I did, and maybe I didn't.

"You ran over the damn dog, you asshole. You fucking killed his puppy."

And if there is one thing that might be worse than fucking your neighbor, this would be it. Fucking killing your neighbor's boy's puppy.

The evidence was there, under the wet of the driveway, a small, dark stain that I swear looked like the shape of a dog, something ghostly in the outline, like what a puppy-shaped rain cloud might look like.

"It was an accident," Melanie said when I went inside, and I wanted to believe her, believe like she did that it happened in that way some things do, not because of anything or anyone; some sort of dark mystery, like the opposite of a miracle. And she came to me and took my hand, the same hand I'd grabbed Sascha's ass with minutes—goddamn minutes!—before. And I let her hold it, because I am an asshole, and I sobbed in the ice-cold foyer of our pretty little house.

"You need to apologize," she said. And, God, I knew I did, there was so much to be sorry for. So I let her pull me over the back lawns and up to Gregory's patio and she knocked on the screen door and cupped her hand around her eyes and peered into the dark kitchen. The sound of Gregory crying was like something boiling. And I stood there feeling sick with it all, wanting to puke. Wanting to run. And the sun burned my neck and I felt eyes on me. When I turned around, there was Dee in our kitchen door, watching. And I looked up, blinking back the tears, and there was Sascha in a window on the second floor, watching. And me in the middle.

"Gregory," Melanie calls into the house. "Gregory," sort of sing-songy.

He comes to the door and he looks shrunken and bloated both, all snotty and red-faced. The collar of his black monkey shirt is wet and tangled, like he'd been chewing on it. Melanie turns the knob and pulls, but Gregory is holding it closed.

"Go away," he says. Quiet at first. Then he says it again, his shrieking voice building up underneath the words. "Go away!"

"Gregory," Melanie says. More cool than a twelve-year-old should be. I am certain I will throw up any second. "Please, Gregory. I want . . ." she stops. "Please. It was an accident."

But we hear him push the lock on the door and he turns away from us and goes back into the dark. Melanie watches until she can't see him anymore.

"Gregory," she says one more time.

When she turns to me her eyes are shining; she is trying hard not to cry, I've seen the look. And she tells me she's sorry. *She's* sorry. Jesus H. Christ. What the fuck have I done? *She's* sorry.

Gregory knew the truth of things, because that's the kind of boy he was, a knower of things. Maybe Sascha told him, only why would she? But maybe she did. Because he didn't talk to Melanie for days, then weeks. And Melanie, once she got over being sad, got mad about that, about how her best friend couldn't forgive her dad for what was not her dad's fault obviously (to her even this was obvious, like so much was to her back in those days: goodness, kindness, evil, pain, fairness). And Dee had taken to sleeping in the guest room.

"The truth," I told Gregory that picnic day in the garage when his mom showed up, smiling. Because it seemed like a good, impressive answer, and I wanted to be impressive right then. Not so much to the little boy, but to his pretty, smiling mom. "Girls want the truth," I said.

So Gregory told Melanie the truth when, after all those weeks, he finally spoke to her again. He came over and the way I heard it later, she was excited, happy they were going to be friends again. And they went to her room and closed the door for a while, and Dee heard Melanie screaming then, and crying, and then there was Gregory coming down the stairs, crying too, and heading out the back door and over the grass to his house.

I got home late from work, like I always did those days, from the tavern really, down the highway where they were building another subdivision. And Melanie was locked away in her bedroom when I got there, and Dee was at the table smoking a cigarette like she never did, and she told me the story and pointed to the bags packed and standing in the hallway.

"She won't believe it," Dee said to me. "She doesn't want to know the truth. There's nothing in it for her. It isn't what she wants."

I'm next to the table and I can hardly stand, not because I'm so drunk, though I am, but because it all weighs so heavy on me. My broken family. The dead puppy. My fucked-up life. My knees are shaking.

Dee is blinking, but her eyes are dry. "I guess I always knew," she says, "but I thought maybe it wouldn't matter after a while. But it does. It really does."

Ten years. And if it made any difference at all I'd tell you about the times when I tried to make it up to them, about stopping drinking, putting money away for Melanie's college, the good things I did out of love or guilt, those two being so close together in my mind.

But what I really want to tell you about is this one time Melanie answered the phone when I called and we talked, kind of. She was eighteen then, just graduated, and filled with some sort of big-heartedness that must have come from her being almost a woman and given, like some are, to forgiveness.

"There's nothing I can say, really, to make it better." I was sitting at the window high up in my studio apartment, the phone so tight to my ear my temple ached. I had a bottle in front of me, newly bought, the good stuff, but I didn't open it. Still, it kept me steady. The city spread out like a board game beneath me.

"That's true," Melanie said. And her voice was a note or two deeper than I remembered it, but otherwise, just the same. A sound that made my throat close. "Is that why you called," she said, "to try to make it better? Is that what you want?" There was music coming from her end, something danceable and familiar, a nineties pop song, I think. I pictured her in the room I'd painted the color of watermelon when she was eight, on the narrow bed with its mint-colored blankets and pillows. We called it her big girl's bed. Only it would have been too little then, I figured out, for the near-woman she had become.

"What do *you* want?" I think I asked her. Deflecting. And even though I was sober then, am sober still, I can't, hard as I try, remember what she said next.

The train pulls into a station and Gregory is standing, and then we are side-by-side. And he urges me toward the door with him, his hand on my back, his litter smell in my nose. The train slows and the low gong plays to let everyone know the doors are opening. He lets go of me and steps down onto the platform and then he looks up at me through his crooked glasses and his eyes are just the same as they were that day in the garage. Big, round, dark pupils. Blue-gray irises.

"Come on," I think he says, but his voice is low, thick, like he never uses it much. And I'm tempted. Tempted to follow him to wherever he wants to take me. To a coffee shop, a park. Hell, maybe to a dark alley where he can kick the shit out of me.

Because here's what I didn't tell you:

My last night in August Orchard, I pull out of the driveway with my bags in the back of the station wagon. And I bounce over the curb, my foot too heavy on the gas, then the brake. And I can see past our house into Gregory's back yard and he's out there on his knees like he sometimes is, in the grass, his hands in the dirt. The little fucker.

I'm out of the car and drunk running between the houses, twisting my ankles in the soft soil, stumbling, but crashing on, charging the kid. He looks up just as I launch myself at him and he's backward on the ground, his glasses thrown and broken, his face white with surprise, with fear. He's a piss ant under me, the cause (I had to believe this) of my little girl's pain, and I push myself up and pull back my arm. I need to hit something.

"Get off him! Get off him!" And Sascha's legs are there in front of me, tan and smelling like coconut oil, but the voice, the yelling is coming from behind me. And it's like my head is filled with water, sloshing around, dizzy and off-balance, and I want to let go of Gregory now, of the T-shirt collar I've got twisted in my fist, but if I do, I am afraid I will fall over. But there are hands on me, on my shoulders, tugging at my arms, and it is Dee now, and Sascha, too, the first time, I'm sure, that they have done anything together since the day of the barbeque, of the puppy. And together they can pull me up and back, and Gregory slides out from under me and scrabbles crab-like across the grass and it's Melanie who goes to him. My Melanie, my little girl. She cradles Gregory and looks back at me and it's all there in her eyes: the fury, the fire, the sharp, dark injury. And before this moment I have never seen her hate anything like I can see she hates me, and it might be the only time ever I know exactly what this girl wants.

And so I leave.

People push around me and out the train doors and the platform crowds with folks going then coming, and Gregory stands there on the platform. "Come on," he says again. And the train empties and fills. The gong goes again, and before I do anything, step off or step back, the doors close and the train jerks away from the station.

And I'm still there, right where Gregory left me.

And I duck and turn to try to see back to the station, to look for my little girl's friend. Only another train is pulling in from the other direction, and there's the signal posts, and the billboards, and the crowds on the way home from work, home to dinner and families.

Or in some cases—mine for example—heading home to our lousy, handmade lives in our lonely, tiny apartments that only offer us the view of the big city, the expanding world, the massive, empty, uncontained sky.

Responsible Adults

Toby said everything would be fine. He said it. They'd been gone days then. Gone a whole box of Cheerios. Gone a gallon of juice. Gone maybe a week. Time was something stretchy to me, long and short, short and long. I was nine then.

We couldn't drive. Not him. Not me. We usually sat in the backseat. Slept there. But when we got up that morning, that first one, the front seat, where they always were, was empty.

"Shot gun," he called. Toby, my brother. Like George always did when Ma used to drive. Back before. When we used to go, when our tires weren't flat, when we had gas, when going was fun still. "Right, babies?" Ma used to say over her shoulder to us when we drove to the river, when we parked near the playground. "This is fun, right, babies?" Leaving. Leaving school. That fleabag—that's what Ma called it—apartment where she and George shared a bed and we got rugs and the floor. Blankets.

Where'd the car come from? I can't remember now. It was just there one day, outside the apartment, Ma behind the wheel, engine going, smoke out its tailpipe. "Shot gun," George called and climbed into the front seat beside Ma. And me and Toby crawled into the backseat on our knees over the spring parts, metal bits sticking up from the cushion.

At night, when we pulled off the highway and into the trees or out in the corn, I couldn't sleep sometimes, and I would stick my fingers in the holes where the springs were. I would dig the stuffing out and roll it in my fingers, make little balls like I used to at the kitchen table with ripped apart white bread that went gray from my hands. "You wash your hands, Tiff?" Ma would say then, mean. Grab my wrists, hard. "Yes'm." A lie. I didn't used to like to wash my hands, didn't like to watch the water, dirty with my skin cells (I remember that from Ms. Garcia's science class from when we went to school) and with whatever was left of what I'd been holding, circle and sink down the drain. Like losing something, I used to think. We never had much. I didn't like to lose things.

Now—ever since we got found—I wash my hands all the time. My knuckles bleed. My palms are raw.

"It's gonna be fine." That's Toby for you, the optimist. Ma called him that. George called him Little Shit. Sometimes it was good, that name, bad words but good in them, like when he, George, first moved in with us, in with Ma, and he would ask Toby to walk on his back. Or when he handed him a juice box. "Come here, Little Shit." And "Here ya go, Little Shit." Those days, the early ones, Ma would look at George with some kind of soft in her eyes and she would run her hand down his face, tuck her head into his chest like she was breathing him in. Pretty quick though, when George yelled "Little Shit," it came out mean, mad. Hard. It got to be more bad than good.

"Hoo hoo," I heard one night in the woods in the car in the backseat. An owl, I thought before I opened my eyes. Because the sound made me imagine something, made me remember. And I remembered, too, from when I was at school, Ms. Garcia would tell us to close our eyes when we wanted to remember something, when we wanted to imagine. Close our eyes when we wanted to see. I didn't understand that at first, and mostly I just saw colors when I squeezed my eyes shut, but sometimes I could see other things. Ma smiling at the kitchen table, coffee cup in front of her, just the three of us there. Toby teaching me how to rub the dirt off the bottom of my feet with my socks before I put them on. A bedroom I imagined was mine but never was, pink and white and frilly curtains.

"Hoo hoo." My eyes tight and there's purple, there's red. And I could see that toy Ma gave me before she took it away. Animals and sounds. Hoo hoo. Meow. Moooo. Owl. Cat. Cow. Owl, cat, cow. Owlcatcow. And George sitting on the porch with a beer and an ashtray yelled like the lion in the toy roared and Ma grabbed the toy from me and smashed it on the front steps and one of the broken pieces hit me in the face and made me bleed a little.

I opened my eyes in the backseat because I didn't want to see that.

And the hoo hoo became "Who? Who?"

It wasn't an owl, it was Ma. "Who will take care of them?" She's whispering, I can hear, though, even from the back seat, even with Toby breathing loud in his sleep next to me. I can hear and I can see, now, with my eyes open, the rips in the ceiling of the car, and the trees out the windows and the shadows and the dark.

"Mama," I say, quiet, because I am afraid of the dark and sometimes afraid of her, too. "Mama?" I say that when I'm happy and when I'm scared, both.

And I sit up and lean over the front seat and I can see them, tangled up, legs and arms and hair and faces. Who's who, I think.

"Shh, honey, shh, baby." Ma unwinds and sits up and next to me is Toby and he's awake now, too. And Ma puts her face close to mine, close enough to kiss, and Toby puts his arm around me and this is good, I think, the way we're all so close, we three. This is how it should be. How I want it to be always. And George jerks his shoulders and sits up quick, elbows popping and his face set hard. I can see his eyes shining at me in the dark.

"It's okay, Tiff," Ma says. She puts her hand on my cheek and her palm is rough and I want it to feel good when she touches me, but really, it doesn't. It's scratchy, her hand. And it smells like burnt things.

"Go to sleep, baby," she says. I nod and Toby pulls me down to the seat and holds me close, his arms around me. I lie there with my eyes open, staring at the place where a light used to be in the ceiling, staring at the way the wires twist and turn, the way they hang down. I can hear what sounds like trucks on the road, but I don't know where the road is, so I close my eyes (purple, red) and listen harder until I can't hear much of anything.

"They'll be better off." It sounds like George, but maybe it's nothing and maybe I'm asleep because I hear an owl, too, so maybe it's a dream or maybe it's a memory. Hoo hoo.

They found us. The farmer first, whose woods we were parked in. Out walking in the early morning and surprised to see me and Toby. "Jesus," he said when he looked into the car windows and saw us wrapped together in the backseat. He pulled a phone from his pocket, spoke quiet into it. "Alone," I heard. "No. No responsible adults." Then the cops came. A man and a woman.

"Tiffany," I said when they asked. They brought blankets and I was happy about that. We were in our shorts, all we had, and our summertime T-shirts. But it was cold now, our breath made frozen spiderwebs on the windows inside the car. I had scratched my name in the fog, in the ice. T. I. F. F.

"Little Shit," Toby answered. Like maybe he'd forgot he was Toby. Like maybe he never really had been. I saw the policeman smile when Toby said that, then I saw him frown.

"Come on," he said. And they brought us from our car to theirs.

I put my blanket over Toby's shoulders. I put my arms around him. I hugged him close and he hugged me back like we did those nights and days after they left. Ma. George. Those days after they were gone.

They were talking in the radio up there. The woman police was at the wheel, the man was shotgun. We could see the backs of their heads and the woods outside the window. It was day but there was dark out the windows, shadows and black places. The woman police turned up the heat. I felt the warm on my face, like Toby's breath at night, only more, and it smelled dry and like metal, not like Toby, moist, animal. The sun shined some through the trees and I put my head under the blanket, squeezed my eyes closed until I saw the colors behind my eyelids. Red. Purple. Imagining, but nothing came.

"Everything will be fine," I heard someone say.
Maybe I believed it. (Red. Purple.)
And maybe I didn't.

Good Men and Bad

I met a man on the road, one of many. I was twenty.

"Where to?" he asked, as most did.

He drove a station wagon. In the rear of it—I know this because I always looked closely at the insides of cars before I got in, clues could be found there: good man or bad? Groceries, good. Filthy magazines, bad. I was usually right—he had blankets and a pillow and a large portrait of Jesus. Blond Jesus, blue-eyed Jesus. In a gold frame, like something you would put over a couch, maybe, or a fireplace. Good man, I thought, although I didn't know for certain. The clues were complicated.

"Next state," I said, hopeful. I leaned in through the passenger side window. I smelled burnt tobacco and sweat and chocolate.

"Git in," he said. "Let's see how far we can git ya." (Git, I noticed. He said it like that: "git.")

"Bill," he said, and nodded some. I saw his eyes then. Dull, yellowed, and gray.

"Dorothy," I said.

"Smoke?" Bill said and pulled a pack of Marlboros from his shirt pocket. The red on the box was greasy with fingerprints.

"No thanks," I said. "Don't smoke."

He turned and looked at me for a second. His eyebrow, the right one, had a scar through it, a white, bald line. Sometimes I asked the men I met on the road to tell me the stories of their scars, but that usually came later, once we'd known each other some. I looked Bill over. He wore suit pants and a white shirt, good clothes—church clothes, possibly (it may have been a Sunday; I don't fully recall) —but they were threadbare at the spots of most wear. Knees. Cuffs. Bill was not an old man, I could tell. His hair was the color of the dirt along the banks of the river where I'd slept the night before, brown and rich.

"Yeah," he looked at the road and slid the pack back into his shirt. "Me neither."

Whose cigarettes then, I wondered. Whose smoky smell? I felt a prickle of something on the back of my neck. It felt cold and blue. (I can feel colors. I've felt them since I was a child in the pitch black of my bedroom: my brother's pure white breathing in the twin bed next to mine. My father's voice felt red, my mother's a watery pink, the sighs between them were silver.) I put my hands on the top of my backpack on the floorboard at my feet. Beneath the flap I kept the Bible I'd found on a park bench, and protection. Nothing much, small caliber. Enough though, I'd discovered along the way.

We exchanged small talk. The weather (warm for autumn), the price of gas (high).

"I can pay my share," I said, in case that was something he wanted.

"No, not necessary. Keep your money," Bill said. He waved a hand between us. There was black in the lines of his palm, dark circles left from old blisters.

"If you're sure," I said. He didn't answer. We rode quiet for a while.

"Been on the road long?" Bill asked after a bit. He eyed me in the rearview.

"Some," I said. "You know," I said. "Just trying to find my way. My place."

"Where'd you come from?"

There was no easy answer to this question for me. Just now, most recently, Missouri. I'd worked the door at a bar in St. Louis, but there'd been some trouble. A few fights. Some guys. I could have told Bill that.

"Out West," I said, though. Because I thought it was a better answer for what he was asking. "My people are from here, though. Family. What's left of them."

We passed a cemetery, with modest stones in rows up a rise of browning grass. Plastic flowers in bundles all over them. A sign at the cemetery's edge was one of those anti-abortion kind. With a baby ten feet high looking over the highway and smiling, shining pink gums and no teeth. "Choose life, Baby," the sign said.

Bill snorted. "Yeah," he said, almost too quiet for me. "Like life's so damn great."

"Got something on your mind, Bill?"

I turned to him and he looked at me. He gnawed on the inside of his cheek; the muscles in his temple worked. He wanted to say something, I could tell. People—men—on the road mostly do talk, I'd noticed. They would say things to a stranger in the front seat of their car they never did before; they would tell things no one else knew. I can't say why for sure, but it happens all the time. It's a phenomenon I mean to study closer someday.

"Nah," Bill said after a bit. He looked back at the road. We drove on without speaking. It was autumn and this was the Midwest and I was glad for it. I loved the gentleness around us, the amber slopes, the long charcoal stripes of highway that split the harvested cornfields, the grassy ditches that trilled with small life sounds. There was not a mountain in sight. I was glad for that, too. I'd been gone too long.

I didn't realize I was asleep until I wasn't anymore. Bill's hand was on me, my knee, and he pressed his fingers hard in.

"Shit," I said before thought came. I struck his hand away. We were driving still, the cornfields had given way to trees, tall and going gold and red. They were fiery streaks through the window and I knew we were going too fast.

"Bill," I said. "Sorry," I said. "You frightened me."

When I looked, he was crying. Tears and snot were smeared down his face. His mouth was open like he might scream; I could see the grayed fillings in his teeth.

"Oh," he said. More like a moan than a word. "Oh."

And he drove faster yet.

There was no one there but us. Not just in his station wagon, but on the highway and the nearby woods. Just we two. I learned as a child how to find animals in the forest by looking for horizontal lines among the vertical ones. Trees rise up, animals run across. I thought I saw a deer in the trees, a long stretch of something tawny. But we were going too fast. It might have been a downed log.

"Bill," I said again. I put my hand on his shoulder, gently, tenderly. I'd done this before. An overture, usually, one of the ways I made money to keep on.

He leaned his face against my fingers, my knuckles. He kissed them, and I let him. He eased his foot off the accelerator some. I turned toward him in my seat, readying myself. I saw Jesus over my shoulder, looking away from us, held in place by gold borders.

When I put my other hand on Bill's thigh, I felt the heat of him, and the sticks of his bones.

"No," he said, and put his hand on mine. "Not that," he said. "That's not what I need." And he hiccoughed a little, a bit of his crying caught in his narrow chest. "Listen," he said, "that's what I want. Just listen." As I have said, men on the road like to talk.

Bill told me. About his niece, whom he'd loved, only unnaturally so. About when he lived with his brother and his brother's family. About the nights he'd enter the little girl's room, hold her when she cried. She was five, six. God, he loved her.

"She lit me," he said. Perhaps he meant that she had "let" him, but it sounded like "lit" and that was most likely true, too.

All the while he talked he stroked my hand on his stick thigh. I felt my skin grow raw under his palm. It hurt to sit there. It hurt to listen.

Did it matter that the girl loved him, too? Bill asked me that. The question sounded well worn, like he'd asked it dozens of times. To himself, at least. Perhaps to others. I don't think I was his first. No reason for that, but I just don't think so. Did it matter, he wanted to know. Because she did, he said. She did love him. She made room for him in her bed. She liked to wash his hair in the bathtub.

And that's when I thought I might be sick. I told Bill so and he looked at me in the rearview mirror, eyes on eyes. "Car sick," I said. But he knew that wasn't it.

"Soul sick, you mean," he said, and wiped a hand across the slobber on his face. He pulled the car over. I opened the door and grabbed my pack and made it to the weeds in the ditch just as I started to gag. Nothing came up. Bill eased the car back onto the highway and hit the gas. The passenger door slammed as he drove away.

A doe leapt across the highway in front of him; I watched. The station wagon screeched and swerved and missed, and then a fawn, small and spotted, was there in the road and Bill hit her. The impact threw her over the hood of his car, then the roof of it, and she tumbled over the blacktop and onto the shoulder. She stood, and I ran toward her, hopeful, ever hopeful (there is so much resilience in the young, after all) but she ran away, her legs buckling until she fell in the grass at the edge of the trees where the station wagon had come to rest too, its front end broken nearly in two against the solid, broad trunk of a maple.

There was silence and then sound. I can never forget that. It comes to me in dreams sometimes, in the glow of my nightlight. It feels thick and purple. I don't know who or what made the sound. It was a wailing, grief filled and sharp. The fawn's mother stood among the trees; I ran; the fawn stilled in the ditch; Bill bled over his steering wheel. The spreading purple noise could have come from any one of us.

I pulled the gun from my pack just in case, but I could see when I was close enough that the fawn was already dead, and mercifully so. I held the gun in my hand and moved toward the car. Bill was alive. Also a small mercy to my mind. Because it seemed to me that there must be suffering in Bill. In suffering he might find forgiveness, I thought. (I was so young, remember, I had not yet finished reading the whole of the Bible I'd found. I didn't know yet how things worked.) In suffering, he might find peace. God. He might find God.

I passed the car and saw that there was blood on the face of Jesus. The gold frame had split apart. I walked on up the road, the grief noise still purple in my ears.

Regarding Alix

I arrived at New Hope Academy on a frozen Saturday morning in early November, mid-semester. It was a temporary gig, a permanent substitute they called it. I'd be there until the beginning of winter break, a little more than a month, while the regular creative writing teacher was out on a complicated maternity leave. It had been a decade since I'd last taught, but after the towers went down two months earlier, freelance editing assignments, my preferred work, were hard to come by. And besides, at that time getting out of my high-rise apartment in the city where planes came in over the lake and circled overhead didn't seem like such a bad idea.

It took six hours in the late fall snow to drive all the way across the state, almost to the river. By the time I got to my cabin on campus, the snow was ankle deep. I was glad I didn't bring much, most of my life was still in the city, so unpacking didn't take long: two suitcases of clothes, another of books, my computer and printer, my cat TJ in his carrier. The cabin was small and cozy, carpeted and wood-paneled and filled with plaid furniture, a real back-in-the-woods place, just like New Hope felt to me. The academy was an expensive boarding school for smart kids, rich kids, spoiled kids. Kids whose folks were diplomats, or were on second marriages and second families, or were high-ranking military officers on the move. Kids who felt more at home in a dorm room with others just like them than they ever did in their sprawling houses with wide lawns and hired help. The academy kept a close eye on these teenagers, gave them curfews and rules, and detentions if they broke either. The school was a dozen miles from the closest town, a few dozen from the nearest city. A safe place, it seemed. A place where planes didn't fly into buildings, where buildings didn't crash down into an enormous pile of rubble. The closest airport was an hour away by car.

I set my computer up in front of the wide picture window that looked over the road toward a two-story cedar-sided building marked "Learning Resource Center." The library. On the second floor, a girl with curly sandy hair and big glasses stepped into the bright frame of one of the windows. She hugged herself, pulled the collar of her olive coat—a man's army jacket it looked like—tight around her neck, and rested her forehead against the glass. She opened her mouth round and blew an opaque circle of fog on the pane. She stepped back, tilted her head this way and that, considered her work, wiped it away with the sleeve of her coat, blew another circle, considered it, wiped it away, blew, considered, wiped. For some reason I couldn't stop watching her, and it wasn't until a campus security guard tooted the horn of his snowmobile outside that I turned away. He gestured for me to move my car and pointed toward a parking lot a few cabins away. I stepped outside and the snow was coming down in feathery clumps, and I looked up toward the library window again. The girl was gone. In her place, a white patch blurred at its edges and then faded to nothing.

In first period Monday morning, two tidy rows held six quiet, pale, sleepy-eyed students. I'd slept badly myself, all that quiet, all that dark. In class I moved the kids in their desks into a semicircle and wrote my name on the board. "Sandy, just call me Sandy," I said, and they stirred behind me. "You say 'Ms. Olsen' and I'll feel like an old maid. You say 'Miss' and it'll sound like you're just trying to butter me up. Sandy. It's okay with me."

I turned to the group, to the boy in the first seat on my right. "And you are?"

"Rob." He had brown bangs down to his nose.

"And you?"

"Madison." She wore a skirt over her jeans, like we used to on winter mornings in the days before they let girls wear pants to school. We'd pull off the trousers in the coatroom, tug on our skirts to get rid of the static cling, slap the white cold out of our legs.

"Gus." Big boy. Broad shoulders.

"Dana." Blond hair cut in spikes.

A girl with too much blue on her eyelids and a thick turtleneck sweater said "Shelly" three times before I could make out the name.

"Elise." Eyes dark and shiny as marbles and a wide mouth.

I ran through the list in my head and matched the names to the class roster I'd pulled from my mailbox in the office. One missing. "And—" I started, but just then the door flew open and a blast of cold air blew in with the library girl in the army jacket.

"I'm Alix," she said, and her voice was much bigger than she was, loud and thick and pitched low. She pushed between two of the desks; snow fell off her shoulders onto Madison, onto Elise, and they scowled and swiped at it. Alix didn't notice. She walked right up to where I stood and handed me a wet sheet of paper, a note obviously, only illegible with its swirls of black ink bleeding and turning gray. "Dropped it in the snow," she said, too loud still, and she sniffed and pushed at her steamed-up glasses and I saw her gloves had holes cut in the fingertips. Her nails were bitten raw and painted purple. "It's from my mom. Sorry I'm late. Snow."

"Your mom," I said, and then I remembered that some of the students were day-schoolers, children of the faculty mostly, or sometimes of the employees—the security guards, lunch ladies, women in the office. They got a break on tuition, and scholarships if their academic records were particularly promising.

"Sandy," Alix said, reading the board. "Well." And she put her book bag on the floor next to her desk still outside of the semicircle. She sat down in the chair and scooted everything up noisily, pushing the desk, pulling the chair, forcing her way in between Shelly and Elise who had to move aside to make room. Alix pulled out a notebook and a purple pen, wiped her glasses with the sleeve of her army coat and blinked up at me. She tilted her head and blinked again, poised her pen over the clean page of notebook paper. Ready and waiting.

"It's the drugs," Dunk, the English Comp teacher said over watery coffee in the pine-paneled teachers' lounge. Jack Duncan, Dunk, the kids—everyone—called him.

For his love of doughnuts and his ability at basketball, he told me. "She's always been sort of goofy, you know, Dungeons and Dragons, Hobbit-y sort of goofy. But now she's a bit of a dope. Doped up." He poured another cup and waggled the pot in my direction. I shook my head. The snow kept falling outside, three days of it now, and the windows over the counter were webbed with frost. The radio was on and quiet voices talked about terror, about revenge, about democracy.

"ADD or OCD or maybe it's—what do they call it now?—not manic depression. Bipolar. Yeah. That's what the drugs are for. That and on account of her brother."

Dunk was my assigned mentor, a fellow teacher who would show me around, answer my questions, fill me in on the procedures. He was white-haired, tall and thin, more legs than body, and a good twenty years older than me. Near retirement, he made sure to remind me, whether the subject came up or didn't. He complained good naturedly about nearly everything: the state of education in the no-child-left-behind age, his wife spending too much money decorating and redecorating their cottage near the small lake just off campus, the neighbors' barking dogs, kids today. We met my first day on campus, and he's the one who told me about Alix's brother's death. A one-car accident two days after the planes crashed, just after the semester started, at the beginning of his senior year. I'd asked Dunk about Alix on this cold day because twice in the past week she'd fallen asleep in my class, come to foggy-eyed and mute when I shook her shoulder, looked around the class like she was lost. She kept up with the assignments, though, turned in pages and pages of highly contrived stories about other worlds and sorcerers and underlings who needed saving and who became saviors themselves. The writing was competent enough, even sort of clever with its complicated plot twists. Still, when we read the stories out loud in class, Gus and Rob doodled elaborate and engrossing chains of calligraphic characters and geometric shapes in the margins of their notebooks, and Madison and Dana and Elise rolled their eyes over and over, so much so they looked like those plastic-headed dolls with wobbling eyeballs that moved in circles when you shook them. Only Shelly listened, tilting slightly toward Alix in the next chair, nodding almost imperceptibly at every turn in the story, tensing her shoulders with any conflict on the page, sighing quietly and satisfied at the story's end.

Twice a week, students could volunteer for one-on-one tutorials with me to go over their work or to talk about their academic plans. Most of my students came once a week at most, answered my questions the way they thought I wanted them answered. "Rising action?" "Through dialogue?" "Description?" Questions in response to questions. I wondered if they wanted to talk about something else. About the crazy world around us, about their folks stationed overseas, maybe about their childhood pets. But most of them, Alix excluded, wanted to stay on topic. "How am I doing?" they'd ask. "My parents want to know if I'm doing okay." "Fine," I'd say. "Tell them you're doing fine." Only how was I to know how these kids were doing, how they were really doing? "I'm not certain," I said once to Shelly when she asked me the standard question. "How *are* you doing?" I asked back. And she stared at me from under all of that blue on her eyelids, and she looked, well, panicked. "'Scuse me?" She said in her quietest of voices.

She tucked her chin deeper into the collar of her ever-present turtleneck. "Fine," I said, and I knew better than to laugh, even though I think I wanted to. "You're doing fine." Relief spread over her features. "We're all just fine," I muttered and shuffled the pages in her folder. After she left my office I locked my door and turned off the light and sat staring wet-eyed in the dark, my throat closing in on itself.

Alix wasn't interested in the writing once she turned it in, and she'd come twice a week to tutorials carrying half-a-dozen books, eager to read various passages to me. "This reminds me of you; it's Nietzsche," she said one day. "'Whoever is a teacher through and through takes all things seriously only in relation to his students—even himself.'" And she smiled and blinked at me through the smudges on her glasses. "Thank you," I said, not sure what to make of it. Alix beamed.

In the teachers' lounge I listened to Dunk's explanation and then carried my mug to the sink and rinsed it out.

I gathered up my papers. "What's the name of that vet again?" I asked as I packed my shoulder bag. TJ wasn't himself. He'd taken to hiding under the bed sometimes, making low, eerie noises, coming out just to sniff at his food.

"Conroy," Dunk said, "over on the highway. Here, I've got his number." Dunk fished the wallet out from his back pocket and pulled out a card.

I made the call from the lounge phone and got an appointment right away. I picked up my things and trudged through the snow back to my cabin.

On my way off campus with TJ wrapped in a towel in the passenger seat next to me, I passed Alix and Shelly at the edge of campus, sitting at a snow-covered picnic table pushed way back in the trees. Their heads were low and close together and Alix held a notebook in her lap. Shelly moved a pen over its pages. Alix looked up into the trees and laughed.

At our next tutorial, I was determined to speak with Alix about the sleeping-in-class situation. I couldn't mention the drugs; privacy issues were supposed to keep me from knowing this. But before I had the chance to say anything, Alix stood up from her chair next to my desk and walked the three steps it took to cross my office and looked at the pictures on my bulletin board. There was the one of my mother and me from the eighties. It was a favorite of mine, both of us in sunglasses and with big hair—hers strawberry blond, mine dark brown—tossing streamers and confetti over the railing on a cruise ship. Another of my ex-husband and me a couple years ago, right before the breakup. I kept it because I liked the way the city skyline made shadows over our faces, over the water behind us. Pictures of friends who were still close but busy, married with children. Black and white shots of my parents from the fifties.

"Your cat?" Alix asked, pointing to one of the photographs. I nodded. "TJ," I said. "For Tom Joad."

"*Grapes of Wrath*," Alix said. "'In the souls of the people the grapes of wrath are growing heavy, growing heavy for the vintage.' I like *Of Mice and Men* better, though. All that Lenny and George stuff. It really gets to you, you know? And my brother's name was Leonard." She kept looking at the picture. She hummed a few notes of something I didn't recognize then said, "You got brothers and sisters, Sandy?"

I shook my head. "I'm an only child. An orphan now really; both my folks are gone."

"Jeez," Alix said and turned toward me.

I waved it away. "No, it's fine, really," I said. "It's been a long time now. My dad when I was about your age, my mom died from cancer a few years ago. I'm used to it."

"Are you currently involved with anyone? A significant other?" She looked at the photo of my ex and me. This was just like Alix. She'd be carrying on a conversation full of shorthand and slang like the other students, and then she'd turn serious. Words she'd read somewhere or heard in a movie came out of her.

"No, I'm alone. By choice at the moment," I said.

"The world is a lonely place."

"It can be. Lonely isn't always bad, though," I said. I was thinking of the way it felt in my cabin in the cool, gentle light of morning. How sometimes on my afternoon walks alone through the woods my heart would expand beneath all the layers of fleece and down, and I'd start to cry for no reason. I thought of the splendid quiet.

"At least you got TJ," Alix said, and she ran a purple-inked finger over the picture.

"I've got TJ," I agreed.

Alix plopped back down in her seat. "Sometimes I think I'm crazy. You know, bona-fide, straightjacket-y loony." Her eyes locked on mine. "But they say it's just a chemical thing. Runs in the family. That's why I'm on the meds." She pulled one of her long curls out from behind her ear and chewed on its end. "And they make me sleepy. Sorry about the dozing off. I'll work on it."

"Anything you'd like to talk about?" I asked. There were whisperings in the teachers' lounge about Alix's brother, about his accident, about how the road was clear when he veered off it and into a tree.

"Nope," she said, and sat quietly, blinking.

Reluctantly, I pulled her folder from the pile of them and slid it between us. If Alix didn't want to talk, we could discuss her work. Just like I did with the other students. I flipped through the pages and looked at the dates scribbled under her name in the purple headings. I chose her latest fantasy world story, although it could have been any of them; they were all more or less the same. "Well, about this piece…"

"You know, I'm not gonna do that stuff anymore. It's so not me anymore. I'd like to try something a little closer to home. You know, write what you know and all that."

"Great," I said too quickly, and she looked at me, a shadow of something in her eyes. "I mean, these are competent—finely tuned, really—stories." I reached my hand toward hers, felt the rhythm of her fingers drumming on my desk. Her eyes cleared again. "But I think you're ready to branch out."

Shelly's tutorial followed immediately after Alix's. I watched out my window as the two passed one another on the sidewalk outside the building, watched as Alix slowed down and as Shelly dipped her head and sped up. Alix's shoulders lifted and lowered, but she continued on toward the parking lot and Shelly came inside, shaking the snow from her hair.

Dr. Conroy found nothing wrong with TJ but said that it might have something to do with being in the country.

"Lots of smells out here, things prowling around. It might be a hunting thing, or a territory thing. You let him out?"

"Is that okay?" I asked, a little embarrassed to let him know that TJ had always been an indoors-only cat, a city slicker like me. Dr. Conroy looked at me. He was an old man with silver hair, pale gray eyes, and skin thin as paper. But he was tall and broad, so he looked strong. Trustworthy.

"He's got his claws. No reason not to." Dr. Conroy patted TJ's head with his big, thick hand.

Back at the cabin, TJ sat in the window and chittered at the squirrels digging in the snow beneath the trees.

"It's cold out there, buddy; you're better off inside," I told him.

Hours later my dreams were full of colors and sound, and I woke up in the dark trying to piece them back together. As my eyes adjusted, the dreams slipped away, but the sound was still there. I could see TJ at the front door in the next room, growling, his tail twitching.

I let him out.

The next morning when I made my way to the kitchen to start the coffee, TJ bounded up onto the outside kitchen windowsill and rubbed against the glass. I opened it wide enough for him to come back in.

Alix's next assignment was just as she said, closer to home. An intelligent, poor, socially awkward girl in a snobby middle school is teased incessantly by her classmates, but she makes a friend, one friend, Sally, a new shy kid who won't speak to her in class or the hallways so as not to be targeted by the cool kids. And this hurts Andrea ("Call me Andy," Alix's protagonist tells the new girl), but she lives with it, grateful to have someone to speak with on the phone, to have sleepovers with, to talk about homework and teachers and the other kids with. Only one day the cool girls, Harrison, Dara, and Elena, catch Andy and Sally talking to one another in the girls' room, and the next day Sally finds nasty notes in her locker. "Loser" scribbled across the cover of her textbooks. And when Andy calls her that evening, Sally won't speak to her, won't even come to the phone. And it is this that breaks Andy. "I couldn't care less what they thought of me," Andy tells her reader, "but Sally, she was something different, you know? In her I could see my future. A future that held others like her, like me, once we got out of this lame school. A future of smart, quiet kids who read books and talked about real things, I don't know, important things. A future of friendships and understanding, away from these overdressed, under-intel-ligent sheep who, for now at least, made all the rules." In the story, Andy exacts her revenge, humiliates the cool kids with balloons filled with paint, and when she's caught, the evidence discovered in her locker, she shakes off the grip of the security guard and marches down the hall toward the principal's office, her combat boots pounding hard on the linoleum. And she sees Sally there, among the faces in the crowd, and Andy winks at her, gives her a tiny tilt of the head. But Sally turns away. "And then I knew," Andy says to the reader, "I was right. Sally was—as much as it kills me to say this—absolutely, totally, completely my future. My horrible, horrible future."

"I am soooo tired of middle school stories," Elise said when we finished reading the piece. She swept her hard gaze around the room at the others.

Madison bobbed her head in agreement. "Oooh, poor little put upon loser girl."

Alix stiffened behind her desk. Her eyes were wide-wide open, watery blue behind her glasses. She chomped on the end of a curl.

"Wa-ah, wa-ah, they're picking on me," Dana said and rolled her eyes at the boys. Gus and Rob snorted.

"That's enough!" I said. And I felt a hot fury rise in me. "How dare you…" I started, but shook my head, turned my back. My eyes stung. How dare they see Alix exposed on the page but refuse to recognize themselves? It was more than that, though. The story, the writing, was good. And I was unwilling to let the personalities of the class run over that.

"This," I said, turning to face them again, shaking the manuscript in my hand, "Is the most sophisticated story I've seen in all the time I've been here. It's not a mall story. Not a broken-hearted teenager story. Not a ridiculous shoot-em-up story." I deliberately looked at each of them. Madison and Dana, the mall story girls; Elise, the broken-hearted; Gus and Rob who wrote about capers and cops. The group fell silent. Alix leaned forward in her seat and stared at me.

Shelly was absent.

I turned toward the blackboard, trembling. "Metaphor," I wrote on the board. "Character," I wrote underneath. "Scene. Story arc." I made a list of all the things I could think of that had to do with writing a successful short story, wrote until my hand was covered with the fine yellow powder of chalk, until the board was full, until my anger was little more than a hot glow in my chest. The bell rang. I waved the kids away without turning around, listened to their chairs scraping over the tiles, their feet shuffling toward the door. When finally I did turn, Alix was still in her seat.

"It's good, you think?" She asked. I nodded. Smiled. She smiled back. "Andy's me, you know. Only with a locker and combat boots." And she gathered up her books and walked to the door. "See ya," she said.

Over the next couple of weeks, Shelly didn't return to class and the other kids tiptoed around me, slid silently into their seats, waited to be called on, slunk quietly out when the bell rang. All but Alix. It was as though she was trying to fill in the empty, quiet space around her classmates. She interrupted them. She interrupted me. Her voice got louder and shriller with every point made. She came to class carrying dozens of books in her arms, dictionaries, notebooks, textbooks, novels, it didn't matter if we were using them or not. She'd dump them all on her desk and they'd skitter out from the pile and bang to the floor, bookmarks and papers and torn pages with purple drawings—daggers and crying eyes—spilling from them. Alix would leave the books wherever they landed, and her feet in their rubber boots would stir through them all during class, melted snow turning the pages gray.

One morning, TJ didn't come home. I opened the front door and called for him, rattled the box of his dry food. That didn't work, so I left a bowl of it for him on the front step and went to class. He wasn't there when I returned that afternoon, but the food was half-gone, so I ignored my growing concern until the sun went down and the temperature with it. I bundled up and took my flashlight and walked the paths and roads around the cabin, calling his name, making kissing noises into the cold, cold air. After an hour, I went back to my cabin, lay down on the couch and tried to sleep. I left the porch light on, and all of them in the living room as well.

In the morning, there was still no sign of him. I canceled all my tutorials over the next week in order to continue the search and hang handmade signs at the grocery store, the post office, the diner on the highway, the photo of TJ from my office under "LOST" in big, black caps. When I was away from the office, Alix would leave one- or two-word notes taped to my doorknob: "Um, well" it might say in purple. Or sometimes, just "Urgent!" Once after class, I stooped near her desk to help retrieve her things. Her wrist was white and stick thin as it extended out from the sleeve of her army jacket. And then I saw she'd drawn a long, jagged, purple line over the vein on the underside of her wrist. I stood up.

"You okay?" I asked. Alix pushed the mass of her hair back, and I could see she'd marked either side of the line with dots. It looked like a scar. She slung her bookbag over her shoulder and shrugged.

"Thanks," she said, and stepped around me.

That afternoon I left a message for the girls' counselor.

"It's regarding Alix," I said into the phone.

"What have you done to these guys?" Dunk asked me in the teachers' lounge. His tie was speckled with powdered sugar. "You should see their essays. Madison's writing about battling an eating disorder. With Gus, it's growing up in a broken home. Rob's writing about running away to

Canada just in case there's a draft. Real stuff. No more crap about peer pressure and the effect of commercialism on Christmas, all that junk they think they're supposed to write but don't really care about."

I shrugged and warmed my hands on my coffee mug. Outside the sun was high and bright. Icicles bled from the gutters. I had hopes that the warmer weather would bring TJ back, but things were looking more than grim. I wasn't sleeping well, listening out into the night for any sound that might be him. I hadn't given a writing assignment in days. We were reading and discussing *The Grapes of Wrath*. Alix had an opinion on everything and argued with anything her classmates had to say. The girls' counselor, in response to my message, left one of her own: "We are monitoring the…situation."

"Shelly's not coming back, did you hear?" Dunk said. "Her folks have been shipped back from their post in the Middle East. Shelly's left for Virginia. She's being home-schooled. They want her to be safe, I heard." He shook his head and reached to turn up the radio to hear a report on the progress of the invasion overseas. He brushed sugar off his tie. "Like it's not safe here," he said.

Tutorials with Alix became painful half-hours of non sequiturs and questions she didn't give me time or space to answer, her voice rising and filling my tiny office.

"My brother told me that girls might have to fight this time around. Do you think Steinbeck meant for the Reverend John Casey to be a Christ figure? You know, J.C.? Sometimes my mom stays in bed all day long."

I began to dread our time together, she was more than I could bear sometimes. And when one evening I saw her in the middle of the road outside my cabin, watching me, I pulled my blinds quickly and stood silently behind them until I heard the crunch of snow that told me she was walking away. Two nights later, Alix trudged up my walk but I pretended not to see her and flicked off my porch light before she got to my stoop.

On a bright, frigid Monday morning after another hard, sleepless night and before class, I drove the half-mile to the grocery store to pick up some coffee. On the way back, I turned on the radio and listened to the news of the world and my eyes burned and filled. In the sharp morning light, the car slipped and slid over the icy road, and I considered for a moment what it would be like to skid into the oncoming traffic or off the road into the trees.

In class, I had the students read silently at their desks while I pretended to go over the quiz from the previous week. My eyes still smarted, and my throat did, too, and the teenaged curlicue script on the papers blurred into shapes and swirls. Alix was quiet for once, but every time I looked up, I caught her staring at me, her mouth a thin, tight line, her forehead creased. The bell rang and she stayed in her seat, hands folded over the open book on her desk. I walked over to her and put my hand on her shoulder.

"I lost my cat," I told her for some reason, sharing my own despair, I suppose. And Alix dropped her head to the desk and howled.

Now here's the bad part. The term ended and with it, my job. Immediately after my last class was over at noon on Friday, I packed my car and drove the two hundred miles home. The city was busy and loud, the sidewalks were icy and salt-strewn, and the gutters were filled with gray slush.

Dunk had planned a goodbye party for me, or his wife did, really, and by the time I pulled into the garage of my apartment building, I knew that the kids and a few of the teachers would be gathering in the Duncans' living room. It was dark, a cold, early winter evening, and I hauled my suitcase and books and the empty cat carrier on the freight elevator up to my apartment. Inside I sat in the dark and looked out at the glowing windows of all the other buildings. I watched the blinking lights of the airplanes that flew low over the great lake a few blocks away.

I should have called someone to say I had to leave early. A cold, I could have said, or a deadline on an editing project. I hate driving in the snow, I could have told Dunk; a storm had followed me most of the way home. But I didn't. I decided I'd send out notes and e-mails the next day, saying thanks, giving students my address. But Saturday my head felt packed full of hot, scratchy rags, and my throat was raw. I slept most of the day. Sunday, too. On Monday I took on the tasks of someone gone too long: called project managers in search of work, balanced my checkbook, dusted and vacuumed. A week passed, and then another.

When I got the news about Alix, it wasn't entirely a surprise. Duncan called, and at first I didn't recognize his voice; two months and two hundred miles made it sound thinner and higher than I remembered.

"Her father found her," he said. "On rounds." She was out in the woods, not too far from where I had seen her and Shelly on the picnic bench, but off the path. Alix's dad was doing what security guards did there, sweeping the woods for kids smoking, making out, skipping class. "Her parents thought she'd been staying with a friend on campus. She'd been gone a couple of days." I heard him take in a long, wet breath. "Looks like she froze," Dunk said. And I said, "Thank you. I mean I'm sorry. I'm—thank you." And we listened to the nothingness on the phone lines between us for a minute, maybe two.

And then I said, "Look. Dunk. I am sorry. You know."

And he said, "Yeah, I know."

And I said, "Look," again for some reason, "I have something…I have to go. I'm sorry. I'll call you back."

"Sure," he said. Not like "Yeah, sure, sure you will," but like "Sure you're sorry, and sure I forgive you, and sure you don't really have to call me back at all." Then he said, "I knew you'd want to know, okay?"

"Okay," I said.

And I hung up.

From my desk I could see the city glowing beneath me, but from here, high above it all, I couldn't tell if it was winter or spring. I thought about the night before I drove home at the end of the semester. I woke up in the dark, sure I'd heard someone outside my window, but when I looked, no one was there. In the morning, though, I could see footprints all around my cabin, small ones, girl-sized ones. And then Alix missed our last class, but I saw her outside the building, under a tree near the parking lot, and she looked in on Madison and Elise and Dana and Gus and Rob. She looked in on me. When I stepped to the window, tried to catch her eye, she turned her back. And later, when I returned to my cabin, the footprints had been wiped away, like someone took a broom to them, swept them off the snowy earth. That's when I decided to leave.

From my apartment I could see the planes over the lake, normal flight patterns and all, and one made a wide, gentle turn and flew overhead. I thought about the passengers on those other planes that September morning, back when the fall semester at New Hope Academy had just begun, back before I got there, back before any of us knew anything bad could happen. Those people on those planes—they had to know what was coming as the towers loomed closer, didn't they? Maybe they could have done something, probably they couldn't have. How many said, "Don't," or "Wait," or "Stop." How many closed their eyes? How many watched?

And yet, none of this matters. It still happened.

Circles, Lake

Sheri hadn't turned away long, it wasn't like that, she'd been paying attention. But, oh, the lake, there under the sun. Sparkling. Glimmering, yes, that's the word. Glimmering. It was morning, early morning, and hadn't she wished she could've stayed in that bed, that big soft bed in the tiny room they'd made her, more like a closet, really, no windows, perpetual dark. And she'd been up all night (most of it, until morning hours, but some would call it night) reading. In the dark of her bed-closet. Because her phone made light, she could read in the dark the small blasts of words her friends from all around the world wrote; read, and look at pictures.

It was the pictures that made Sheri turn from Hope, her charge. Three and willful, the little girl was too stubborn to ride in the stroller. –Walk!, she'd hollered, face puffy with sleep, yogurt crust at the corners of her mouth. –Lake!

Sheri let her walk. Held her hand as they crossed the busy road from the condo to the lake, busy with cars on their way to work, impatient and honking and glinting under the bright sky. Jealous, Sheri was certain, of the slow stroll into the perfect summer day she and Hope shared.

To the lake, morning-empty. The lake with that glimmer and swoop of gulls overhead. Perfect. Perfect. Calm here, despite the wind. Sheri pulled her phone from her back pocket, held it between her face and the view. The sun made it hard to see the screen; she pressed the button again and again, trying to get it all. She heard the quiet slip of water, like a fish turning, maybe (she didn't know, she usually lived in New Hope, far away from this great lake across from the condo where Hope had lived with her parents who worked, both of them, who hired her, an au pair they said, and it was just another thing that Sheri both loved and hated about them, the way their money made them a little snooty. Show-offy).

And then she saw the man in the air, flying. An immense, curved kite lifting him up and up, over the water.

—Look, Hope, look, Sheri said and pointed with one hand, pushed at the camera button with the other.

—See? And she turned to where the little girl, her charge, her responsibility, had been sitting on the lake walk a minute—no, a second!—before, drawing circles on cement with a chalk she always carried for these purposes.

Only the circles were there, blue like water, like sky, wobbly drawn, overlapping, making one shape into another when you looked at them just so. The chalk, abandoned now, in the middle of the smallest circle.

—Fuck. Shit. Sheri said the words and felt them in her stomach, in her chest. She whirled in her own circles. Behind her, the morning commuters honked and honked. Before her, the lake glimmered and glimmered. The sun hurt her eyes.

Kitty

The power had gone out. And I'd lost my keys. That's the kind of day it had been.

The city is crazy dark when the power goes; my headlights made ghost tunnels down the street—gauzy, glowing columns. In my periphery, I saw movement, or thought I did. Shadows wavering, black against gray. Candlelight here and there in the windows of buildings. Flashlight.

Mel was a week gone, and I'd only just got out of the apartment after days crying under the blankets, mascara and snot streaking my pillowcase and his, what used to be his, the one that still held his smells—sweat, garlic, coffee—even though he'd packed his bags and a few boxes and taken the French press and left. Left me, left Kitty.

And it was Kitty that finally got me out of bed, out of the apartment, because she was hungry, we'd gone through the cans of meat for cats, of tuna when the meat was gone, the bits of fish and cold cuts and cheese and yoghurt and milk that were left behind in the fridge. Things Mel bought because I didn't cook and sometimes forgot to eat and had charmed him in the beginning of things (when we fell in love at the park where I walked Kitty, so small then, a dozen pounds and just to my knees, on a lead every morning) by confessing that my favorite meal—breakfast, lunch, dinner—was microwaved popcorn.

We were even out of popcorn.

Kitty had climbed on me fetal-folded in the bed, on Mel's side, where I imagined his skin cells, miniscule flakes of them mixing with mine and clinging to me like flour on a dredged chicken breast. And maybe, after four days without food and cried out, I was hungry, too. Like Kitty. When she moved, the bed dipped and I rolled toward her, and I loved the feeling of her ribs expanding under my palms, her fur, her warmth. She put her muzzle to my face and made a sound like a snarl and her breath was bad, fetid, sour milk and dead things.

The power was still on then and I walked to the bathroom and Kitty padded along beside me, nudging my hips with her noggin like cats do, licking my fingers (for the salt, I suppose, poor hungry girl) and the backs of my knees. I showered and dressed and went out with wet hair and no makeup, in jeans and a hoodie, because, really, what did it matter? And the drive to the store was easy and quick, the sun sinking on the horizon, the sky going gold, then purple. At the store the aisles were empty (Monday night football) and when I got back to the car it was dusk and I couldn't find my keys.

I shifted the bag (heavy with cans and a cooked chicken in a plastic tray because Kitty would like that) from hip to hip while I searched my pockets and the ground and went back in the store where no one had found them and everyone (clerks, customers, the homeless guy selling papers near the door, the men in oil-stained pants who always sat on the bench by the parking lot) shook their heads sadly and looked at me with big wide eyes shining with pity. My chest ached. My face burned. I felt a buzzing across my scalp.

Good luck or bad, Mel lived a block from the store and I knew he had keys still because he hadn't left them when he left me, left Kitty, and I hadn't asked for them because—well, just because. Hope, I guess. And I hoisted the bag and the chicken smelled greasy and good and I thought I would call him, but I'd gone out without my phone. I could picture it on the bedside table next to the tissues in the box and in soggy balls, next to the water glass that Kitty drank from more often than I did, the phone's little green eye staring back at me when I checked it again and again for messages, for texts, for missed calls, and found none.

So I stood on Mel's stoop and rang his bell and imagined his surprise when I said into the intercom, "It's me."

"Uh," he said, or that's what it sounded like and I waited for the buzzer to open the door, but instead here he came down the stairs in bare feet and jeans and buttoning his shirt. I watched him through the door glass and even from there I could see the scratches on his face, on his neck, welt-y and red, and I swallowed hard when he pushed back his hair like he always did, first thing in the morning and last thing at night.

"My keys," I said when he opened the door. "I've lost them."

"Okay," Mel said. And he waited there with the door open but not wide enough for me to come through. Up close I saw how the skin puckered around Kitty's marks.

"Um," I said. "You still have a set."

And he looked puzzled, his forehead lined, and nothing in his brown eyes.

"I think," I said. Even though I didn't just think, I knew, I knew. I knew because he hadn't left them, he'd taken them when he left, and I wanted him to know that, to have done it on purpose, left but not gone, the keys a way back. To me. To us. To Kitty.

"That cat," Mel used to say, but not in a good way. And Kitty, stretched long between us in the bed, paw to foot, eye to eye, her meaty foreleg across my neck, would snarl a little at him and hiss. "Someday," Mel used to say, "you're gonna have to choose. Me or her."

But I never thought he meant it until he did, after she ripped his bathrobe to shreds, standing on it and tugging the arms out of their seams while he watched from the bathtub, chest-high in water. And she bared her fangs when he stood up, dripping and shaking and naked. And there they were when I came home that day two weeks ago, Kitty on the bath mat, her three-foot-long tail swishing, her eighty pounds of fur and muscle vibrating, her purr audible from the front door, a motor in a barrel. And there, too, was Mel, blood on his face, on his neck. Naked still and cupping his privates, protection, I guess, his skin a little pale, a little blue.

"I'll look," Mel said and left me on the stoop for a minute, then five, and the evening was warm and full of football-on-the-television noise and talk and cheering and booing, and it smelled like burned leaves (and greasy chicken).

"They were in a box," he said when he came back down the stairs. "I guess I was in a hurry." And he dangled them on the chain with its tiger eye marble medallion we'd bought at the zoo. Apartment keys, car keys. Everything I needed.

"Thanks," I said. And I smiled at him (because he always told me he liked it when I smiled) and wished I'd put on makeup and a sexy blouse, the one the color of a panther, maybe, with the deep slashed collar.

He nodded and we stood there on either side of the threshold.

"Which one's yours?" I said. "Apartment, I mean," I said.

"Second floor. Front," he said.

And I stepped back some on the stoop so I could look up to the window and there it was, bright and open, with blue curtains that moved a bit, then closed, and someone was in there and my heart hurt and a cat, a little one, a kitten really, palm-sized, leaped up onto the sill and tilted her golf-ball head toward me and opened her teeny-tiny pink triangle mouth and meowed, only I couldn't hear it, a silent meow.

"She followed me home," Mel said when he saw what I saw. "So I let her in." And the heat rose in my forehead and stung my eyes from the inside and somewhere, at the edge of things, everything went dark.

One block had lights and another didn't, and then another didn't, and then another. And I drove around for a while seeing only what my headlights showed me but knowing there was more.

I parked finally, two blocks from home because that was as close as I could get. And the sidewalks were ink-dark and there weren't even stars and the bag was heavy and I could hear things in the grass, in the trees, and my face was wet, but I tried not to sob.

Behind me, footfalls. Not steps exactly, but more like the sound of Kitty prowling at night in the hallway—up and down, back and forth—and around the bed. And breath. I heard breath. A wheeze. A purr.

I walked faster and he (she? It?) did too, and I opened the door to my building and climbed the stairs (five flights, elevator out) in the pitch-black dark and on the landings I swear I could hear lips and tongues together, on skin, the sounds of love making or eating. And behind me on the stairs, breath still, and climbing.

She followed me home, Mel had said; I could hear that, too. Still.

At my door I leaned my forehead to it and said, "Here Kitty, here Kitty," quiet, like pillow talk, and I could hear her in there, paws, claws, on the other side, as high as my throat.

The climbing behind me had come to a halt, but still there was breath. And the cans in the bag rattled when I turned the key (Mel's key) in the lock, and the chicken in its plastic tray made a sound like a slap.

"Here, Kitty," I said again, into my unlit apartment, and I stepped inside and felt something soft underfoot, a shredded rug, I think, the stuffing from the couch.

I turned back toward the breath and it came closer and it stank, like garlic, like coffee. Like Mel.

"Come in," I said, and I felt Kitty's tongue, (like love) heavy and wet and sandpapery on my elbow. Her purr went low, thick as a growl.

"Please," I said again to the breath in the dark hall, "won't you come in?"

Serve and Protect

Truth is, I was never much good at my job. Serve and protect. Serve and protect. Yeah. Sure. But how?

Like that time I was out on the highway. Early morning. Bad mood. My wife Ellie and me, we'd been on the phone the night before. Our anniversary and her a state away. City sounds over the wires. She said some things. Me, too. Bad things. You never. Your fault. Names. I don't want to say. Wouldn't let me talk to Robbie. Wouldn't let me talk to S.J. Sure, I'm drunk. Sure, it's late. But still. Not like that's my thing, drinking, got that mostly under control. But like I said, it was our anniversary. She was gone. They were. I was alone. I said some more things.

And that night, noise in the street. Kids, cars. It's summer, sure, but maybe it's more than that. But I'm drunk. Like I said. I ignore it. Or maybe I passed out. Can't be sure.

I should've known better. Mad, tired, hurting from the drink, but out there in the morning anyway. Because I had to be. My job. What I do.

This guy, this brown guy, out running. I'm thinking, who? I'm thinking, why? Like I'm supposed to. I turn on the cherries. Pop the siren, just a blast. The guy jumps, like maybe he hadn't heard me before. Jumps. Misses a step.

Falls. I hate to say this, but I'm thinking a brown man on his knees in the middle of nowhere looks guilty as hell.

It's just a couple years since those towers went down. Brown guys did that. That's what I'm thinking. Mad still about Ellie, about our phone call, about not being able to talk to my kids. S.J. Little Roberta.

Serve and protect.

"Stay down," I tell him. I got my hat on. My hand on my holster. It's dark yet, that early. But there's a line of light on the horizon. Pink. Gold. Most mornings that's all I see out there, that's what I watch for. The sun. The next day.

He turns a little, but on his knees still.

"Hang on," I say. I'm not scared. He's small, it looks like, him on all fours like that. I can take him. He's not wearing much. Shorts. Sneakers. A gray T-shirt. Wrinkled. Like a runner, though. That's what he looks like. Long brown legs. Bandy. And then, shit, I know. I know. But here I am, on a different path already, following the wrong signs. That's what Ellie always used to say: You look for the clues, but you miss the signs.

Running shorts. And not just sneakers, but good running shoes, thick rubber soles, expensive. Not like from the Walmart over by the river. Still, I can't be too careful. That's what I tell myself. Even though I know. Serve and protect.

"Morning," I say. And because I know, my mad has shifted some from Ellie, the phone call, to me. This guy. This poor guy.

"Morning," he says back. But he's looking at the ground between his hands. Head down. I'm close enough to see now he's got blood on his knuckles. Scrapes. The fall. My mad is leaking like air out of a balloon. I'm so tired.

"Okay," I say. "Easy now, get up easy." I'm trying to sound firm, but not like an asshole. In charge, though. And he does just what I say. Sits back on his heels. Rolls his shoulders. Stands. Turns. All real slow, just like he knows I want. He's taller than I thought, taller than me. Stringy, muscled rope, though. I still think I could take him if I needed to. Don't think it'll come to that, though. I'm not so mad anymore.

"Early, isn't it?" I say.

"Yes," he says. He's a good looking fellow, even I can see that. Dark hair, dark eyes. Like that guy on that cop show that Ellie used to like. The guy and the show.

"I.D.?" I say. Because I can tell he won't talk much. Not like he's scared of me. It's not that. More like he knows how things will go.

"Sorry, no," he says.

"Really?" I say. "You don't have identification?"

"Not on me," he says. "Just a morning run. I like to keep my load light."

His knees are bleeding. Scraped up kind of bad. He doesn't sound fully American. Some kind of accent. But still, I know. I know who he is.

"New in town?" I say. Not wanting to give away too much. Wanting him to take responsibility here, too. You can't come into a new town where you don't know anyone and run around in the dark without I.D. You just can't. Especially if you look like this guy. Time was, these fields would be full of men who looked like him. Planting, picking. You could hire one or two for not even a living wage and because the locals didn't want to do that work anyway. We all had jobs then. Two factories, shops in town, road crews, three schools: grammar, junior high, high school.

The courthouse. Things to do and we were the folks to do them. The fields were for farmers and farmhands. Hard workers and cheap labor. Now, though, the corporations owned a bunch of the land. They had massive, expensive equipment, combines and tractors, pickers and irrigation rigs. Things I don't know what they do. But I do know it only takes a couple guys to run them. Now the fields were full of machines more so than bodies.

"New in town, yes," this guy says. Looks right into my eyes. Says no more. The sun is behind him now, coming up bright. I try not to blink. I'm getting a little booze-woozy.

"Address?" I say, wanting to speed things up, get to a john. And he tells me. The old Paper House. Where Doc Paper used to live. Biggest place in town, empty for years. None of us could afford it, afford the upkeep. This guy, he's the new plant foreman. Down to one plant now after all the layoffs, and the company hires an outsider to run things. People are pissed. I've heard them. At Jack's Supermarket, at Charlie's Tap, at Supples Supper Club.

"Okay," I say. And because I've come this far, "Got someone to vouch for you? Call your wife, maybe?" I've seen her around, and those kids. She's pretty, blond and pale. Those kids, the little one, a little younger than S.J., cute as hell. The girls pretty like their mom and dad, both. That older boy looks like his old man. They just moved in, but her and those kids have been coming around for a couple months now. Checking things out. I can't help but notice, because of my job, maybe. Because of them, probably. Not like the rest of us, quite. Not that that matters. I know what this sounds like, but I'm not prejudiced. I'm not.

"Our telephone isn't hooked up yet," the guy says. Of course. Of course not. We stand there still, and it's like we're sizing each other up. He's not afraid of me. I like that.

"All right," I say after a long minute. "You're bleeding," I say. "I got a first aid kit in the back of the cruiser." We walk together, and when I pop the trunk, I get a small hiccup in my chest, like a warning. But I ignore it because I know it's wrong. It feels different when it's right. More urgent. Not dull like this. Maybe something to worry about, this feeling, but nothing to be afraid of. I can't explain it quite. But I turn my back on the guy and get the kit and hand it over to him.

"Thanks," he says. But he just holds it. Doesn't open it. Doesn't get out the Bandaids or the alcohol wipes. He rubs his bloody knuckles over the front of his shirt.

"How about I get you home," I say. And he looks over my shoulder at the long road he'd been running and I can tell he wants to get back on it. But I can tell, too, that he's not stupid, he knows what's good for him.

"Sure," he says, and it sounds a little funny. Like choor. "Thank you," he says like he's just then remembering to be polite.

We get in the car after a second when he hesitates at the doors on the passenger side.

"Up front," I say, trying to sound casual, like there was never any other choice. I open the windows because I stink and he does. Booze, me, adrenaline, him. My stomach tilts. I pull a u-ey near Jack's Super and there are trucks already at the bays. Lettuce from California. Corn from somewhere else. Then we're at the driveway of the House of God. He puts the first aid kit on the floor at his feet, dips down a little and looks past me and up the Hill.

"Big church," he says.

"Our biggest," I say.

And then we're quiet to the stop sign, quiet after the turn toward town. Quiet still when we pull up and his wife, the pretty blond lady, is out on the stoop with a broom and a frown. There's trash in the street, on their wide, sloping lawn, trash on their sidewalk. He gets out, leans in, says thanks again. Polite, like I say.

And it isn't until I pull away quick, wanting to get home for a pitstop and then the diner for coffee, and see him in my rearview mirror, blood on his shirt, watching me, his wife watching him, the trash from the kids the night before all down the green hill of their front yard, that I realize I never asked his name. Policing 101. Get the name. Well, shit. I forgot to ask his goddamn name.

The Truth Is Not Much Good

"Tequila," I said. "Two, please." I pointed to the pint bottles behind the counter. Guillermo smiled at me. A nice smile. A come-here smile. We'd stopped for gas and for beer. Toothpaste, because neither of us thought to pack any.

Once we were told there was no real proof, no evidence, just her word against his, we'd left the kids behind, Ramon in charge, Paco in his crib, the twins already deep in a movie, *Princess* something. I didn't know it, the film, but I knew, just from its stupid title, that I hated it. Girls and princesses, something so precious about that. So contrived. But they were all there, our four, home and safe. We didn't worry, not now. It would be all right. They would be fine. What—after everything—could happen? The worst was over.

I don't remember whose idea it was to take off like this, to get away—his or mine. Drive up the road toward the river, stay in the Motel Six there. We, like everyone, had heard the latest about that girl, our neighbor's daughter, and the lies she'd told. And not just this time. It seemed like a good idea to go now; the snow had slowed and the highways were plowed.

At the Stop & Go one town over, the woman at the cash register barely looked at us. I don't know if it was because we were different, Guillermo and me, light and dark, or if she recognized us. Guillermo wasn't in the paper, we had that at least to be thankful for, but there was that list girls—women—were adding to. With pictures, too. On Facebook, on Twitter. That hashtag. I could feel the woman's disapproval of us, thick as it was, like fumes in the air. It had been a while since I'd seen this, the way people could hold love against you. We paid for our gas and grabbed the beers and the tequila and went back to our car. "Bitch," I said and turned the engine over. Guillermo put his hand on my knee, gave it a squeeze. Through the window we could see the woman watching us now, her arms crossed over her chest, her face pinched. I thought, or maybe I imagined, I saw her own wedding band, thick and gold, the flash of a diamond on her third finger. What, I wondered, was her marriage like? Was she happy? Were they? What secrets—the wobbly foundations we built our unions on—did they hold, together and alone? What did she know for certain? What did she suspect? I pulled the car carefully out of the lot. There wasn't far to go, but the road in the dark was tricky, shining with ice under the streetlights. Things looked ridiculously bright; everything made my eyes smart. We passed houses glowing with Christmas lights and decorations, and we commented on it, "Huh, look at that," we said. We'd forgotten that it was nearly Christmas. The red and green and gold strobed over our windows, flashed over our faces. I kept my foot lightly on the gas and my hands tight on the wheel. It took nearly ten minutes to drive a single mile, slow and steady, and at the county's only stoplight we slid some in the intersection. When we took the next turn into the drive of the Motel Six, the tires slipped and grabbed all the way up the hill to the parking lot. There was a minute just near the top when I was sure I felt us pulled backward. Guillermo caught his breath and I could hear him whisper, "Come on, come on, come on, come on. Make it. Make it."

We didn't have much. Clean underwear, toothbrushes. And now beer, tequila, toothpaste. A plastic bag. My purse. The motel was empty, off season and the storm. The lobby smelled of cooked cabbage, and when we checked in, we could hear children laughing through a door behind the front desk. We took the room furthest from the lobby, on the second floor at the end of the hall. We locked the door. We were thirsty from relief and desire, so we drank and we fucked. And after, we opened the second bottle of tequila and drank some more.

"I'd like a cigarette," I said.

"You don't smoke," Guillermo said.

"No. You're right. No." Did he hear that thing in my voice? That thing he used to comment on: a tone or a catch or question that made it sound—Guillermo said—like I was trying to convince myself of something. He used to joke that the first time he heard it was when I was pregnant with Ramon. We were still in Honduras where we'd met, me just seventeen and there on a church mission, until I lost my faith—and not for the last time—and left my friends and my host village and hitchhiked until Guillermo found me on the side of the road, sunburned and blond, not like anyone he had known before. "A vision," he sometimes said. "A goddamned vision." And when I got pregnant, Guillermo asked me to marry him. "Sure, yeah," I'd said years ago. Something like that. "You don't sound too eager," Guillermo had said.

"No," I'd said. We were in bed when he'd asked me, in a tiny room in a guest house in Tegucigalpa. The windows were open and a noisy, metal fan on the dresser stirred the heavy, moist air.

"Yes, I mean," I'd said then.

That's the way we told the story for a long time, to our kids, to friends and strangers at dinner parties, at cookouts. We laughed over my "No," over my "Yes." Which was it?

"I am eager," I'd said finally back then. In the small bed in the little room in a country I had lived in for just a few difficult months, I took Guillermo's hand and put it on my belly—right where Ramon was growing. I pushed it lower. "Let's get married," I'd said.

"Have you ever?" he asked from his side of the Motel Six bed.

I looked at him. We'd left the curtains open, no reason not to. No one was out there, no one could see us up here. Night and street light came in through the window, watery Christmas colors at its corners.

"Smoked, I mean," Guillermo said. "Have you ever smoked?"

We'd been married nearly twenty years. Had he ever asked me this before? Did he really not know?

"Yes." I pushed myself up in the bed, pressed my back against the headboard. I still had my bra on, but that was it. The bra was for him. Guillermo liked it when I wore just a bra, this one particularly. From one of those catalogues, midnight blue and silky. I'd thought of that when we'd packed, when we thought, finally, everything was okay. I thought of him.

I drank from the tequila bottle, felt the good burn of it in my throat. I handed it to Guillermo. He drank. Coughed. Cleared his throat.

"When? When did you smoke?"

"Today," I said. I held up a fist, raised a finger, counted. "Yesterday." Another finger, another. "Day before."

"Oh, come on," Guillermo said. He sat up, too. He seemed a little shaky, though. Drunk, maybe, some.

"Oh, come on, yourself," I said. I could hear the small slur in my words, drunk myself some as well. "You really don't know?" I said, trying to make out his eyes in the shadows. "You really never noticed?"

Guillermo shook his head.

"No," he said. He shook his head again. "Guess maybe we do have some secrets." He'd denied that before, just a couple of days ago, when the cops showed up at the door, when we saw that neighbor girl watching from her bedroom window across the street.

"Some," I said.

And maybe this was the time, I thought. The time to tell him. About after Ramon was born, after the girls.

"I need a cigarette," I said. He laughed, rolled his eyes. "No, really," I said. "I'm not kidding."

I got out of bed and put on my boots and my coat, hugged it tight around me. Guillermo watched me as I walked to the door. He watched me open it. He was watching me still as I closed it behind me.

The parking lot was a sheet of ice. I slid and my coat flew open and the frozen night air hit my almost naked body beneath it. It felt brutal. Harsh. Like a punishment, like a penance. I yanked the car door open, my fingers ice-burning on the handle. I rooted my cigarettes out from under the seat where I kept them hidden, and I skittered back across the lot. One bright window in the entire hotel, ours, and Guillermo was up there, looking down.

When I came back into the room, he rubbed my icy body. He warmed me up. He loved me, I could tell. Still. Yet. I stepped out of my boots and dropped my coat on the floor. We got back into bed and sat in the dark.

"Yes, please," I said when Guillermo offered me the tequila. I drank. I lit a cigarette. Ashes fell on my bra. I brushed them away and could see how lines radiated from my cleavage over my skin. It looked old, my chest. Ancient.

"You didn't smoke when you were pregnant, did you?" Guillermo asked. His eyes moved with the cigarette. To my mouth, to the empty beer can I used as an ash catcher on the bedside table. To my mouth again.

I shook my head.

"Good, because," he said. But then he stopped. I knew what he was going to say. I knew it. I said it for him.

"The miscarriages," I said. Gently. Cautiously. *Cuidado, marido,* I thought. Be careful, husband.

I drank the tequila bottle empty. *Cuidado.* I put it down; I stubbed out my cigarette, lit another. I blew smoke. Then, "They weren't all miscarriages," I said. "Not that first one."

Guillermo stared at me, and I stared back, unable to speak, to move. The cigarette burned my knuckles.

"Shit," I said. "Ouch," I said. I dropped the thing into the beer can and we were so quiet, so very quiet, we could hear the tiny sizzle of it in the beer and backwash at the bottom. I stared down at my old, old chest, the wrinkles over my ancient heart, and told him.

I could not stand it, another child. We had three already, and they were needy, so needy. When I'd told Guillermo

I was pregnant again, I thought he would feel as I did, unable, overwhelmed, not ready. But he was thrilled, like he was the first time. And then the second as well, which, because they were twins, was both the second and third. I took care of the fourth one on my own. And I lied. I told him—told everyone, because everyone knew I was pregnant, my folks and his, our friends, even though I hadn't said anything to anyone besides Guillermo—it happened another way, the loss. I pretended that it had. I pretended it wasn't my fault, that it was beyond my control. I even cried a little, don't ask me why, I wasn't faking it, not that. And Guillermo was good to me then, as he always was. Kind. Tender. And sadder than I had ever seen him. And I felt horrible for what I had done. But truth? Good, too. I felt relieved. Free.

I told Guillermo all of this in a bed at the Motel Six, but I did not look at my husband while I spoke. I felt him beside me, felt the waves of sorrow lifting from him. I heard him whimper. I heard him cry. I could have—should have—reached for him then. But I didn't. I kept talking until I'd said it all, until there was nothing more to say. The room was hot and dark and smelled of burnt tobacco; I'd smoked all of my cigarettes.

"And the others," Guillermo said, bracing himself I saw. Holding the sheet in his fists.

"No, God no," I said. But why would he believe me? Why should he?

"That was different," I said. "I was ready. We were. The little ones weren't so little anymore. You had a good job." Why had I smoked all my cigarettes? Why was there no more tequila? I pulled the tab on another beer. It was warm and tasted like spit. "Guillermo, I wanted another child.

Our child. I don't know why those others didn't work. I don't know, maybe it was because of…because of…" I drank from the beer. "When Paco was born we had grown up. I was grateful for him. I fell in love immediately. That's all I wanted. From the beginning. To be in love with all of our children. But, damn, Guillermo, we were kids at the start. Just kids ourselves."

I was hoarse from whispering. Who would hear us? We barely—and this was not new—heard one another.

"Let's sleep," Guillermo said when I finally, finally stopped talking. He slid deeply under the blankets, hot as it was. I went to the bathroom, peed, washed my face and hands. I didn't turn on the light. In the mirror I was just a black, empty shape.

When I climbed between the sheets Guillermo's back was to me. I could barely hear him when he said, "You didn't believe me."

"Hmm?"

"About her. The neighbor girl. You didn't believe me." His voice sounded wet and broken. "What does that say about your feelings for me? What does that say about us?"

"No," I told him. "You've got it wrong. What does it say about me, my not believing you? What am I capable of?"

But I knew, and now he did, too. I was capable of deceit. I, wife, woman, was capable of harm. And here is the shit truth of it, the shit truth of me: since I was capable of these things, these terrible, terrible, selfish things, I was willing to believe that Guillermo, Guillermo, my good, right, honorable husband, was capable of them as well.

"I didn't do anything," he said. He wouldn't turn around, he wouldn't look at me. "I could have," he said. It came out pointed, sharp. I deserved it. "I was tempted if you want to know the truth."

No, I thought. *I don't want to know the truth. The truth is not much good.*

"But I didn't," he said. "I never."

"No," I said to him. "Shush, now. I know. Shush." I put my hand on his neck; I kissed the spot between his shoulder blades, I kissed a knob of his spine. "Shush." I needed him to stop talking. I needed to not hear anymore.

The crash woke us up.

"What the—" Guillermo said. He sat up in bed. I did. Groggy. Not yet sober. We stumbled out from under the blankets and ran to the window.

There were two cars at the bottom of the motel entrance, way below us. One was nose up against the telephone pole, the other one was smashed into its tail end. The drivers were out of their cars and on higher ground, up to their knees in snow, waving their arms and yelling. And coming around the bend in the highway, was another car. Slow. We watched as the traffic light went green to yellow and the car, still coming—down the slope now—picked up speed. The light went yellow to red. The car kept coming. We watched, we and the drivers. The noise of the crash was sharp in the frozen, clear night air. Then it went silent.

"Holy," Guillermo said.

I put my forehead against the window pane. I felt the cold of it all the way to the backs of my teeth.

"Look," he said. And around the bend there were lights flashing, a cop car making the curve. And the guy in the third car, the driver, got out of his vehicle and did a dance to keep standing, his feet moving on the ice. And the police car followed the path of the third car, and probably the second, and the first. Sliding, sliding, toward the three cars, toward the man. And the third driver stood still, next to his open door. *In or out*, probably, the guy was thinking. *Stay or go.*

"Stay," Guillermo said. He put his hand on the back of my neck.

"Go," I said, the word a white circle on the window.

We watched as the police cruiser seemed to aim for the crashed cars and for the man.

"Shit," Guillermo said. And it sounded like it hurt him, the way he said it, strangled, tight. The way he said it hurt me. "Yes," he said, yelling then. "Go! Go! Go!"

And it was like the man could hear my husband, because he looked up and at the same time pushed against the door, gained some ground underfoot, made it to the other side of the road just as the cruiser barreled into his car.

The heater clicked beneath the window. Guillermo put his arms around me. I felt his body against my back, the warmth of it, the familiarity of it.

"That was close," he said into my hair.

"Yes," I said. "That was close."

"Glad it's over," he said.

"Yes."

We pretended not to see the next set of headlights as they shone around the bend.

"Close the curtains," I said, my back to the window. Guillermo tugged them shut. "Come to bed."

He did. And we lay together in the dark, holding one another, holding on. The sounds of tires on ice and of metal on metal did not stop for some time then, and we could see the trails of emergency lights at the edges of the window. We ignored it, though, the damage outside our room. We had to.

.

A Good Reader

No one knew me there, two towns away, brought to this place in the cars of strangers. I did this sometimes, walked to the highway at the end of my mother's road, exhausted and yearning after days with me and Mom, just the two of us. Her needs, my duties. But on Wednesdays, the Angel Helper would come, take my place at her bedside, shoo me away. "Go," she'd say. "Relief," she'd say.

This time, a bookstore. I'd been here years before the illness brought me back to my mother's house, away from my suburban life where bookstores were big and noisy with coffee makers and children running in the aisles. But when I stepped through the door I was the young woman I'd left behind when I first left home. I breathed in the scent of the place, paper and ink and dust and chamomile and the slight, not unpleasant odor of cat kibbles. I filled my lungs with it and remembered:

How I'd sit cross-legged between the stacks, books scattered at my knees. How I'd read and get lost in the words, the smell, the quiet. Once I met a boy here, I remembered that too. He commented on the title in my hands, turned the pages to his favorite part near the end. I could smell the Prell in his hair as he bent over my lap. He left before I asked his name.

This time, a young man behind the counter. Tall and reedy, graceful. Curls and a scraggly red beard, round wire glasses. Just my type when I was his age, a dozen years ago. In his hands that same book, from that boy time. *Ulysses.*

"I love that book," I said. He looked up, surprised to see someone there. His mouth was lovely, full lips over slightly crooked teeth. I could see pocked scars in a small circle under his ear. He blinked.

"Joyce," I said. And he said, "Philip." I shook my head. "James Joyce," I said, pointing. "Not me." And he smiled a little, reddened a little. "Oh," he said.

"I've forgotten my glasses." Where did this come from? I don't wear glasses. "Would you mind? My favorite part, the end? I would love to hear it out loud."

He looked embarrassed, uncertain. He was a clerk after all; this—what I wanted—was not his job.

"I promise," I said, "I'll buy that book, and at least two more." On the counter were cannisters with coins and bills: *Reading Series,* on one, and *Fluffy Food Fund,* said the other. A picture of a cat on a pile of books, her tail slinking down their spines. "I will make a donation," I said.

He nodded and I said, "Last pages. Start with '. . . *my God after that long kiss I near lost my breath yes he said . . .*'" I spoke from memory. Philip moved around the counter, leaned against it. I sat on an overstuffed chair with sagging, orange cushions, slipped my shoes off and curled my legs underneath me, my heels tucked under my bottom. I could feel my pulse in the soles of my feet, in my lower parts. I pulled a throw pillow embroidered with golden flowers over my lap.

". . . *my God after that long kiss . . .*" he began, his voice barely a whisper. Raspy.

Could he see me rocking?

Outside it was a sunny day, "'... *hid for her lover to kiss ...*'" The blue sky shone in the windshields of the cars parked along the sidewalk. Outside people passed and looked at their palms, read from small screens.

"'... *or shall I wear a red yes and how he kissed me under the Moorish wall and I thought well as well him as another ...*'" Philip's voice was low now, urgent. Could he hear my breath quicken?

Two towns away, the Angel Helper read A. A. Milne to my mother. *Now We Are Six,* her favorite book from childhood. "'... *I asked him with my eyes to ask again yes ...*'" I would buy *Treasure Island* for her today, another favorite. I was certain this bookstore would have it. I looked around at the orderly and packed shelves, rocking, rocking. They had everything. "'... *I yes to say yes ...*'" I would not be disappointed. This kind of place would never disappoint a reader.

"'... *and first I put my arms around him yes and ...*'" I knew this part, I recited with him, rocking on my heel under me, rubbing against it, with it. "'... *drew him down to me so he could feel my breasts all perfume yes ...*'" I pressed hard on the pillow in my lap, imagined the golden flowers moving over my skin. "'... *and his heart was going like mad and yes I said yes I will Yes.*'" "Yes!"

We got to the end together, our words in tandem, full-throated. Breath and joy and release. Relief.

He looked up from the page and I didn't look away. I didn't bother to pretend that I wasn't flush, I wasn't sweating, I wasn't panting. What is that old joke? What does a woman look like when she is satisfied? This, I thought, the waves ebbing inside me, the thrum and twitch slowing.

This is what she looks like. My friend, dear Philip, pushed his glasses up his nose and smiled at me, stepped back around the counter and slid the book into a paper bag. I untangled myself and bent to my shoes; I could smell the tang and yeast of what we'd read rise from my flesh.

Treasure Island, Mrs. Dalloway, Their Eyes Were Watching God. And something new: *Sing, Unburied, Sing.* I piled the books on the counter and slipped a twenty into the reading cannister and another in Fluffy's food fund. I handed Philip exact change for my purchases.

"Thank you," I said. "My pleasure," he said. And I thought, but did not say, how the pleasure was all mine. Because he knew that. He was a good reader, after all.

I walked the main road to the highway and when I saw the glint of sun on the grill of an approaching car, I put my thumb out. I hugged the bag of books tight to me. I could feel, I swear, the rhythm and breath of their words upon my skin.

Yes I said yes I will Yes.

No Worries

You'd think he'd be too old for this sort of thing. Hell, that's what he thought.

He'd met her in line at the shop, flustered and digging in her bag, looking for the extra bit of change to buy milk with, just a little jug, enough to pour in her coffee, she said, talking to no one, to everyone, looking around and smiling at the clerk, at the woman in line a few folks back, at Jim, there directly behind her. "Sorry," she said. She said it to him, and he nodded a little like you do if you don't just look away, don't pretend it isn't happening, don't ignore someone else's embarrassment.

"No worries," he said. Why'd he say that? He never said that. His boy said that, only he wasn't a boy anymore but a man now, off in the city, working long days for his family, his wife and little girl. But when he was a teenager, Danny, Jim's boy, said that. About everything. "No worries, Dad," when Jim got on him to help his mother with the shopping, to get at those weeds in the garden. "Sure, Dad, no worries." He was a good kid, Danny was. And when Rachel died and Danny came back home from university and missed his exams that year, he said it again, "No worries, Dad." And together they went through Rachel's stuff and sorted it out and tossed some, papers and old photos of family members neither of them knew, and took the rest—clothes, bags, shoes—to the charity shop. And then Danny went back to university and then to the city where he got a job, got married, and so on.

So most days, especially now that he wasn't working anymore, a pensioner—how'd he get to be that old, he wondered—Jim spent on his own, and he liked it that way. Quiet. No one bothering him or needing anything. Not like Rachel had been particularly needy, but those last years, when she got so sick and barely recognized him and couldn't do anything for herself anymore—cook, get dressed, bathe—well, now not being needed was a bit of a relief. Long morning walks through town, a stop for the paper and pleasantries at the shop. Enough to keep Jim going, to feel something other than utterly alone. A routine. A ritual.

But there she was, this one, the lady with the milk, throwing things just a little off. And why was that? Something in her face, maybe. Her eyes. Brown and soft. Kind? When was the last time Jim thought of that word, kind? Kindness. And so he slipped a hand in his pocket and pulled out a pound and put it on the counter in front of the woman. "Let me," he said, and smiled at Alan behind the till same as every morning, and he smiled at the woman, too, and said again, "No worries."

She waited for him outside the door and made him promise that she could make it up to him. "A drink," she said. And he could see the top of her head when she bent to write something on a small slip of paper, and there were gray hairs among the brown ones. She looked up again, handed him the paper with her name, Dorothy, and a number, the name of a café. "Yes?" She said. "Say five o'clock?" She was American, he was pretty sure, even though she hadn't talked quite enough for him to know, to place the accent, but he was pretty sure anyway. He didn't know a lot of American women. Saw some on the telly, though. Smart, mostly.

He'd bought a new shirt, only it had been so long since he'd bought anything new, and before, it had been Rachel who did most of the buying, so he got it a little small, a little tight around the middle. But it was bright white and sharp, he thought, when he looked in the mirror, smoothed down his eyebrows, plucked a couple of hairs out of his ears. And he sucked in his stomach and headed out the door for the café. It was just half four, and the place was close, but he didn't want to be late; Jim was not one for lateness.

He got there early and stood for a bit, at the door near the tables outside. He saw his reflection in the window and stood up taller, but thought he looked silly there, standing, shifting foot to foot. Where should he put his hands? So he sat, ordered a glass of wine, waited. And she, Dorothy (he said it to himself, a rhythm in his head, "Dorothy, Dorothy, Dorothy"), was late. And that's when he thought what he thought, that he was too old for this. This—well, whatever this was. Meeting somebody. Buying new clothes. Waiting. He could be home now, sitting alone, with something cold from the fridge, some crisps. That was good enough for most days, should be good enough for today.

His palms were wet and his shirt was tight and he was just about to pay up and go, ten past five already, but then he saw her, Dorothy, hurrying around the corner, head down and feet quick and light on the pavement, her skirt dancing around her knees. She wasn't young herself, but she had a nice figure, Jim thought. She looked up and he saw the line of her neck stretch from her jaw to her collar and he felt something like a shock, a spiral of something electric, something warm, something good.

"I'm too old for this," he muttered to the man—himself—reflected back from the window. And he nodded at the reflection and pushed up from the table and turned to Dorothy just as she reached the café and she lifted her face to him, her cheek to be kissed.

"Here goes," he thought, "no worries."

And Jim bent down.

Maria Concepción

This is where I found her. In His church, my church, one early winter's morning not long ago, curled up on a pew, weeping. She had no coat, and her dark hair was wet and white with snow; her clothes, a pair of Levi's and a sweatshirt with the logo of a community college across the river, were soaked through. The storm outside was not a blizzard, but close enough. The poor girl could have frozen.

"Hello," I said that morning, dark still, but bright, too, from the snow on the ground, in the air. The church windows were mostly clear (except for some small stained-glass panes, the Virgin Mother, the baby), and tall and wide, made to look out on God's splendor up here on the hill. They were filled with winter's image. Shadows draped the chapel; I'd be lying if I said it wasn't a little frightening—this girl, what could be seen and not.

She didn't answer me. Her eyes—that particular jewel color of some people with dark skin, topaz and circled in black—glowed with her tears and something else, I would know later. She shivered and sucked on the collar of her sweatshirt.

"Hola," I said. "Que pasa," I said. My Spanish was limited, mostly high school lessons and phrases we used to say to sound cool: que pasa; que vola; comprendes? Back then it was mostly us white kids in classes; the migrant workers came to town alone for the field jobs or if they brought their kids, it was summertime so no school. And while we locals all went to the public pool to cool off and swim, those other kids went to the quarry. That was their place, an unwritten agreement. But sometimes some of our boys got a little drunk or high or bored and drove out there to make trouble. It isn't all that different today, I'm told. The troublemakers breed I suppose.

But this girl. Coatless and wet, she was in my church, my home (I have rooms behind the chapel) and she needed help, I could see. Warm, dry clothes, maybe food, a place to sleep, possibly.

I gave her all of these things. And on that first day, a Monday, she stopped crying, but she said nothing. She took the hot bath I drew for her and ate the eggs I made and wore my flannel nightgown fresh from the dryer and slept on the couch in my office under a blanket. I worked around her, did my books and read my Bible and drafted my sermon like I did on every Monday. I would try to push through an entire first draft if I could chase the inspiration left over from Sunday service and the previous week's observations: a car stuck in the snow, a conversation overheard at the post office, black squirrels under the trees. I never knew when something would click, something would take hold. I had to sit at my desk, pen at the ready, journal open, write one sentence and the next, start and start again. On this particular Monday the words were hard coming. Outside, it snowed and snowed.

Tuesday morning, the girl was awake before me. I smelled coffee and toast as I sat up in my single bed (bought on mail order when I was newly alone), as I whispered my day's greeting to God. Shadows and low golden sunlight touched the corners of my room and my stomach spoke to me. I slid into my slippers and robe and made my way to the kitchen.

I've always loved this room, my kitchen. *Always* meaning the two years I have been the pastor of this congregation, and the twelve years before that when my husband Oliver was. I am not old, just forty-three, but I am a widow, a senseless drunken driving accident having taken my husband from me—from us, his congregants, the town—just down at the bottom of the hill where he'd driven one late night to get the milk I'd forgotten from Jack's Super up the road. I was already in bed by then, like usual. I had left Oliver in his chair in the living room as I often did those last months, watching the news and muttering, smoking, filling his glass. The sirens made me look up from my novel. Oliver was gone barely a half-hour by then, I wasn't worried, not yet. Someone would always slow him down, stop to make small talk or big talk (he was a man of God, after all) and Oliver, even on these muttering, drinking nights, took time for others. One siren then another, and I picked up my phone on the bedside table and switched it on. Back then I would turn it off at night, night calls only brought bad news and bad news was Oliver's business, not mine. Back then. A flood of texts filled the small screen, the volunteer fire brigade's chain of response: *one car accident. bottom of the church hill. Jack's Super. ambulance.*

And still, even with all of these clues. Let's just say that some things were beyond my imagination.

The girl spoke that morning, but try as I might, I couldn't understand her. We sat in my favorite room with its yellow-painted walls and shining appliances and windows that looked out towards the nearby woods. The squirrels made circles in the snow, foraging, searching. Behind my chair, on the wall, golden haired Jesus stared upwards, framed in plastic. This was Oliver's choice, his favorite Jesus image; I'm sure you know it. Blue eyes, white skin. I always thought Jesus would be dark-skinned, given where he was born; I preferred to think of him that way. I knew very little about genetics then (and still) but I understand now that things don't always come out as you think they might, as you think they should. With my back to the wall, I didn't have to look at the golden Jesus, but I kept him there to honor my late husband. This room, my yellow kitchen, is where Oliver came to me still, where we communed sometimes in the early dark of the morning, in the late dark of the night. "I miss you," I would say. "Me too, you too," he would answer. I swear that he would.

The girl talked and talked that Tuesday morning. She looked over my head at golden Jesus and smiled. "Concepción," the girl said among the words and sentences she'd let fill in the air around us, between us. Concepción. The word in her language was prettier than in ours, like most words are, I've noticed. I thought it must be her name. They had names like that, didn't they? Things we didn't usually call our own children. (I don't mean me here, I don't have children. We never did.) Concepción. Angel. Jesus.

"¿Ingles?" I said finally, after I'd eaten my toast and had my coffee. After I'd grown tired of nodding and smiling, nodding and smiling. As you do.

"No," she said, smiling back at me, shaking her head. She looked happier than she had when I found her. Perhaps it was the warmth. She ate her own toast dry; drank tea with milk, lots of milk. "Not much," she said. And I knew she meant not at all. She was just being polite.

"I like her," Oliver said.

Although I told her it wasn't necessary, the girl helped keep house, dusting and mopping and scrubbing the tub, those things I mostly let go now that I lived on my own, now that I had a job. My taking over the congregation was not something I strived for, nor even actually applied for. I was qualified, Oliver and I went to seminary together after all, but when the board asked me to stay on, to step into the role of pastor, it was not because of my qualifications. It was because they knew me, I was from here. Thirty years ago my folks moved us to New Hope, so I've been years here. Not as many as Oliver and his people—generations buried in the cemetery overlooking Market Street—but enough that people consider me a local. I imagine that's why they gave me this job. With me, they knew what they were getting. (So they thought.) And I, too, accepted out of a same sort of familiarity, a certain sense of complacency, an unwillingness to start again, start somewhere else. And because Oliver was here, still, too. I don't believe in ghosts, but he was here still. Of this I'm certain.

Concepción and I navigated the first week with a series of hand gestures and lots of pointing and nodding and speaking slowly. We began, ever, ever so slightly to understand one another. I think this must be at least in part because I listened to her, really listened. This isn't my strongest suit, listening (I know, that's a troubling confession from a person of the cloth), but something in her voice made me want to hear what she told me, to avoid my habit of believing I knew what was going to be said, to think I knew what would come next. And, too, Spanish is a language that makes sense to me, unlike some I have heard. Czech for instance, the language spoken by the landlord of our first apartment when we were newly married and finishing our degrees; Dutch, what my great grandmother spoke when she came to visit us from the Netherlands one time before she died. I began to recognize some of Concepción's words. Almuerzo. Hace frio. Tengo sed. Cocina. Buenas noches.

She called me Alicia, another word that was prettier than the one I used: Alice. And when I called her Concepción, she would laugh and laugh, and put her hand on her belly. I didn't know what was so funny, but I laughed along with her. It feels good to laugh. Who would deny that? Sometimes in the yellow kitchen I would hear Oliver laugh with us.

Sunday, then, and Concepción was among the few in the pews. I would like to think that it was the snow, nearly a foot and more predicted, that kept people away, but that would not be entirely accurate. We are a small town, New Hope, getting smaller all the time. And we are a town of many churches, five besides mine. Competition is stiff. You might think our lowering attendance had something to do with my being a woman, and perhaps it did some, but even when Oliver was alive our numbers dwindled.

I smiled at my congregation, welcomed them into the warmth of the chapel, the warmth of His love. That was my theme that day, something about warmth and love. It seemed appropriate when outside the temperature was dropping and the roads were turning to ice. People listened (I think) even as they fiddled with the hymnals, stared out the windows to the trees thick with snow and the black squirrels beneath them. Only Concepción watched me as I sermonized, her eyes glowing, her hand on her belly, and it was then that I understood what I hadn't yet. The girl—because she was that, a teenager and no more, surely—was pregnant.

"You're pregnant," I said to her when the service was over, after everyone had climbed into their cars and driven down the hill toward the icy highway. We were in the yellow kitchen making tea. I hoped that Oliver might visit me then, might give me some guidance. Concepción smiled at me, her whole face aglow, but she did not understand, I could tell. "Embarazada," Oliver, close by, whispered, reminding me of the funny Spanish word that sounded like something shameful in English. Pregnant.

"Si," she said. "Yo se," she said. And laughed. Always—except for that first day when she cried in my pew—Concepción was inclined toward laughter I couldn't help but notice. "Te lo dije. Immaculada Concepción." And it's true, she had told me. But I'd misunderstood. I understood now, this time, but only her words. The rest baffled me.

"Como te llamas," I said.

"Maria."

"Maria? ¿Por qué?" But that was as far as I could go. Por qué. Why didn't you stop me from calling you Concepción? Why didn't you tell me, really tell me? Why do you think this is an immaculate conception? Why are you here?

"It's all right," I heard Oliver say. "It will be fine." And the kettle whistled and Maria Concepción prepared our tea and she smiled at me and her eyes looked golden and the snow started up again and we sat in the yellow room listening to the radiator clank and hiss and deliver its warmth.

"Who is this girl?"

I had to consider my words carefully. I was prone to lies, a habit from years past when Oliver's sadness grew so thick, when his drinking became a problem. But it was a habit I was trying to break. It exhausted me sometimes to always ask for God's forgiveness for such things. It occurred to me that one day His forgiveness might not come.

It was our monthly board meeting, and despite the snow and the cold, we had a quorum. Three of them and me. We sat circling the conference table, the radiators rattling around us. Snow melted in pools from the boots of the men; the only woman besides me had slipped out of her galoshes at the door.

"Her name is Maria. Maria Concepción," I said. "She came from across the river. She helps me in the house, she cleans the chapel." True, this was all true.

"Is she legal?" one of the three asked. I won't tell you their names or details; I don't want any trouble. I knew what he meant, though. New Hope is nowhere near a border. We sit in the middle of the country, close to the wide river that cleaves the land in half. And yet, some of my neighbors struggle with the idea of who comes and who stays, with the promise of a wall still unbuilt, with a yearning for a country that never was as they believe they remember it. I am trying to be delicate here. These are my neighbors.

"Of course she's legal," I said. And this was not a lie. All humans are legal, the way I see it. Whether Maria had documents or not, I wasn't sure. But to me, that didn't matter. Still, I understood why it might to them. We all saw the news. We remembered the boys in the quarry when we were just kids, the others more recently. We heard about what happened two towns over at the Iglesia Hispaña when they took all of those people away as they left the service. Fathers, mothers. Children.

"She used to be Catholic," Oliver said to me, his first time in the board room with us. I repeated it. "She used to be Catholic," I repeated, and added, "But she has doubts."

Now this was a lie, or perhaps not. I had never asked Maria Concepción what her faith was. But I knew this lie or truth would work in her favor with the board. They always kept tally: how many of them, how many of us? It was a matter of numbers. It was a matter of acquisition. It was a matter of sides.

"You may stay," I told Maria Concepción. "As long as you want." We were moving her things (flannel nightgown and robe, jeans and sweatshirt, a new winter coat, three dresses, very stretchy yoga pants and oversized T-shirts, a Spanish-English dictionary, fluffy slippers with cat faces over the toes) into my bedroom so she could have the real bed. Her belly and back needed comfort my office couch couldn't give her any longer, big as she was becoming. I didn't mind. Oliver had taken to visiting me in the office as well. In fact, this move was his idea. "Give her your bed," he'd said to me that morning when I'd come in to the room to bring her tea, saw how she winced and struggled up from the sagging cushions.

"Gracias," Maria Concepción said to me, and took my hand. She opened my fingers and kissed my palm. "I will repay," she said.

"No, no," I said. We made the bed up between us. She folded the corners of the sheets and tucked them in tightly, hotel style, military style. Where had she learned that? "Nothing to repay," I said, and slid a pillow into its case, plumped it at the head of the bed.

"Yo insisto," she said.

The next morning was a church day and our numbers had grown. The pews were filled with Spanish speaking men and women, children. I didn't recognize them, although there was something familiar in their faces; like perhaps we had met briefly once, or passed close to one another. I couldn't quite put my finger on it, and after a while I started my sermon (coincidentally about community and welcome) and stopped thinking about it. Maria Concepción sat in the middle of them all, and I saw how these new congregants yearned toward her, how they touched her shoulder, her head, and later, when we gathered for coffee and cake, how they rubbed her belly and kissed her palms. Her topaz eyes glowed and glowed.

"Well, well," Oliver whispered to me. He was in the assembly room now, with the rest of us. I stood near the coffee urn and felt him close, but I didn't know what he meant. "Well, well, what?" I said. But he didn't answer.

"Do you know these people?" I asked Maria Concepción later when we sat in the yellow kitchen, eating leftover sponge cake and drinking milk. She looked up from her plate. There were crumbs in the corner of her mouth. I reached across the table and brushed them away.

"People?" She dabbed her lips with a napkin.

"Today," I said, "at the service."

"No," she said.

I leaned back in my chair, took a sip of milk, looked at Maria Concepción. Her belly seemed to have grown considerably in just a couple weeks' time. It pushed up against the edge of the table. She looked over my head at golden Jesus on the wall.

"They seem to know you," I said. And she nodded, still gazing at the portrait.

"Yes," she said, and yawned. I sat listening for more, but that was all she gave me.

"I think it might be true," I told Oliver one night when I couldn't sleep. Two more weeks had passed, and even more people came to the church each Sunday. Standing room only, and everyone (not just the Spanish speakers) wanted to stand close to Maria Concepción. The few families and widows and widowers who had attended services since way back when, during Oliver's tenure and after, the ones who used to scatter themselves over the pews as though they wanted the chapel to look fuller, bunched together in the first few rows behind Maria Concepción. The board members jockeyed for space in the pew next to her. I saw her smile and glow at them when they reached toward her; saw how she guided their hands to her middle. "Why can't it be true," I said. "Stranger things have happened." Oliver and I used to say this to one another often in his last months when the perilous tilt of our country and the world beyond filled me with wonder, him with dread. "Stranger things."

"Yes," he said, but that was all. I turned over on the couch, listening to the radiators and Maria Concepción's quiet snoring in the next room. Outside I heard what sounded like a car; I saw the pass of headlights throw columns over the ceiling and walls. The church stood high on a hill, away from everything, what would a car be doing up here at night? By the time I got to the window, it had turned back onto the drive. It looked like a black sedan. I thought I saw the silhouettes of two people, but I couldn't tell for certain. The car moved down the icy drive toward the highway below, its taillights glowing red. Nothing to worry about, I thought.

"Stranger things," Oliver said then.

The following Sunday the parking lot was full; people squeezed together so everyone could fit inside. It was nearing Christmas. I know that is quite the coincidence, but it is true. The winter's day brought more snow, and an ice storm was promised by midnight. I looked out the kitchen windows toward the trees and the logging road beyond. I had begun to wonder if anyone cared what I said these days, or if they were all just here because of Maria, because of what she brought to us. We never spoke of it again, not she nor I; I told no one (besides Oliver) what she claimed. I never heard her tell anyone else.

I left my spot in the small room behind the chapel, that place I stood each Sunday and gathered my thoughts, where I watched people shuffle into their pews, where I could see and not be seen. I went back into my yellow kitchen and drank a glass of cold water to clear a small tickle I had in my throat. Out of the window and among the trees, I thought I saw a man. Was that a man? Oliver? Of course my heart went there, but I knew it wasn't Oliver. Oliver was not an apparition, after all, he wasn't a ghost. He was a voice. A knowledge. More than that, although I can't explain this, he was not a vision. The man in the trees was there and then gone, and I heard the sound of an engine before I saw a car moving along the logging road.

"It's time," Oliver said to me. And I went to speak my piece.

"Jesus said, 'What is impossible with man is possible with God,'" I said, looking out at the packed pews and people standing in the aisles. There were more new faces. Toward the back of the room stood a couple of burly blond men. Maria Concepción, sitting on a cushion in the front pew, smiled at me and nodded. "Amen," she said.

"Amen," the room responded.

The ice came earlier than was forecast. The last of the congregants had barely made it to the highway when the sky turned the color of slate and the fluffy, wafting snow turned to furious pellets of sleet. They battered our windows and pinged on the roof. Maria Concepción and I sat in the yellow kitchen. She stared over my head to golden Jesus on the wall behind me. I thought her eyes had lost a little glow, but perhaps that was the darkness coming in from the outside. "¿Cómo te sientes?" I asked. She smiled at me, but not quite as usual. Her lips trembled and tightened. That's when her water broke.

"Dios," she said. "Ohhhh, dios…" It came out part moan, part prayer.

"It's fine, just fine," I said. I was up on my feet, then down on my knees near her chair. I put my hands on her face. "Look, look at me," I said. She did, but her eyes were wild with pain. I helped her up and to the bedroom, cooing what comfort I could think of in Spanish, in English. "Calmate," I said, "You're all right." I had no idea what I should do.

When Oliver told me in his last months that he was afraid of the ways of our world, that he felt, despite his work, his job, unable to help anyone anymore, that he felt futile and impotent, I didn't listen. Rather, I suppose, I listened, but I didn't hear. It wasn't the first time, exactly, that his doubt and despair got the better of him. He leaned toward sadness often. It was part of what made him so good at what he did: empathy. Or so I thought. I am not saying that his death wasn't accidental; I don't believe it was intentional. But I also think that when he saw it coming—the drunken slide off the church driveway across the highway and against the tree beyond—he may have welcomed it. "Listen," he'd said to me before he went out that night, an icy one just like this one. He stood in the doorway to the bedroom. "Hmm?" I said. I didn't look up from my book right away, and when I did, finally, he was already gone.

"I'm listening," I said to the doorway. Maria Concepción was crying and laughing and murmuring. I could not hear what she was saying, but it wasn't her words I was listening for anyway. Oliver, I needed Oliver. He would tell me what to do. He would tell me.

I'd already called for the ambulance, and I heard the sirens somewhere, not particularly close. The roads were treacherous, I knew, they would have to go slow. I had my hands on Maria's knees; we'd moved her to the bedroom. She pushed back up against the headboard and made a low moan, and in that instant, her baby was born. You hear these stories sometimes of quick and easy births, and you wonder if they are true—or perhaps it's just me who wonders, never having been a mother, never having wanted to bear a child. But let me tell you that in this case, the story is true. There he was, covered in the muck of his mother, squirming and ready for breath. And it was as though Maria Concepción had practiced for this moment. She reached for the child between her legs and pulled him to her gently, careful of their cord. She ran her finger around in his mouth, she patted him and he cried. I brought towels and hot water, because that is what they do in the movies, on television, and she took these from me and when the water had cooled some, Maria cleaned her child tenderly.

"He's beautiful," Oliver said, finally, finally. And it's true, he was. Not in the same way as his mother was beautiful, dark and glowing. Instead, his hair was curly and golden, and his eyes, when he opened them, I knew would be blue.

"Don't cry," Oliver said to me. I didn't know that I had been, but I had.

When the knock came on the door of our rooms, I went to it, ready to let the paramedics in. Only it wasn't the paramedics. It was a man I'd seen earlier at the back of the chapel. Big and blond. With cold blue eyes.

"We're looking for Maria—" and he said a last name I hadn't heard before. Behind him was a black sedan, idling in the parking lot. Another blond man sat in the driver's seat.

I shook my head.

"No," I said. "I don't know that name." This was not a lie.

"Close the door," Oliver said.

I stood staring at the man. He looked mean and hard as solid ice. He stared back at me. Those eyes. Those blue, blue eyes.

"Come on now," Oliver said. "Close the door."

"Yes," I said to my dead husband, and the ice-cold man looked confused, surprised. "You can't be here," I said to the blond man, because in that instant I believed that was true. Whatever would happen later didn't matter just then. Not in that immaculate moment. "Close the door," Oliver said once more. I did. From the bedroom down the hall came a small whimper, a quiet laugh.

"Yes," I said to Oliver again, "Yes, I heard you."

At the Corner of Cole and Porter

Was it always like this? Edna couldn't remember. She couldn't remember much these days. Like: Who was the Secretary of State? When was Alaska named a state? What was another name for the War Between the States? When did her house get into such a state? That used to help, mnemonic devices, like things. State. State. State. Now, though, not so much.

Where were her keys?

Dorothy, her daughter, worried. Edna knew that.

It was Monday. Maybe. Was it Monday? And there was Dorothy in the foyer between the doors, front, dining room, living room. Edna remembered this.

Dorothy, eleven then, that other time. There were the four of them, Edna, Ed (people called them The Eds. Edna liked that at first, being half of something that deserved its own article: THE Eds), Edna, Ed, Dorothy, and Davie. They'd just moved in to the big house on Cole Street. From the front porch you could see the street signs, Cole, and the cross street, Porter. Wasn't that funny? Edna remembered that, too, there was something funny about the street names together like that, Cole, Porter, but now—how many? Forty-five? Fifty?—years later, she couldn't remember what was funny, why it was funny.

Where were her keys? "God knows." She hummed a little and words popped in her head: "Anything goes." She riffled through the pile-up of purses on the piano bench, heard Dorothy tapping her toes on the parquet floor of the foyer, heard her daughter's huff of breath, heard her sigh.

That's how Edna found her then, way back when. When? The day they moved in and there were boxes, so many boxes, piled high on the porch, in the foyer. And the children, Dorothy, Davie, were loving it, the mess and play of moving, of change, of new. Circles. They ran in circles like dogs on short leashes strapped to a tree. Front door, dining room door, living room door. In out in out inout inout inoutin.

It was too much. Ed, working, always working, never home. And the running, the yelling, the boxes, the heat (it was summer then. Too darn hot, Edna hummed, sang in her head, Dorothy grown now and sighing. Edna opened another purse, green and the size of a briefcase with golden buckles and a zipper that had pulled away from the leather—was it leather? Real leather? Too darn hot) and so on moving day fifty years ago, Edna tucked away in the kitchen, on the cold side of the house. The north side (or was it south?) and let the door swing shut behind herself, sat for a while on the cool wood-planked floor, rested her shoulders and head against the low cupboards, closed her eyes.

The green purse was not empty, but it had nothing in it. Nothing that mattered, anyway. Used tissues, a few pennies (she wondered what year they were from, featherbacks? Or that new image, what was it?). She couldn't see well enough to make out anything but that they were dull and brown and round.

"Ma?" Dorothy called from the foyer. "Ma? You okay?"

That was a battle long lost. "Don't call me Ma," Edna always pleaded, "you sound ignorant." When had it gone from Mommy to Ma? "Okay, Ma," Dorothy used to say. "Sure, Ma." It started as a joke, a ribbing (but a little mean, Edna thought, mean like girls could get). Dorothy was sixteen back then and coming into her own, a woman sometimes, a girl the rest. It stuck, though. Ma did. Woman did.

Davie—her favorite even though she wasn't supposed to have favorites, but she did, everybody did Edna suspected, liked one better than the other—Davie had always called Edna Mother.

"Mother!" Edna didn't know when she fell asleep, didn't know how long it had been. Where was she? Here. On the floor of the kitchen. Here, by the cupboards. Here in this old house, but new to her, here on the corner of Cole and Porter. Moving day. Forty-five years ago. Fifty. "Mother!" Davie's face was dirty, play and summer dust (it didn't rain that summer, Edna remembered that) and from his crying he had white streaks over his cheeks. "Come," he said. "Come." He pulled on her, his hot hands in her armpits.

"What," Edna said. That day. Back then. Groggy. Foggy. Stuck somewhere between dream and real.

"Ma," Dorothy said. Now. Here.

In the brown purse with the copper beads sewn along its seams Edna found peppermint candies wrapped in plastic. She used to take this purse to the movie theater when she and Ed had their night out. "Here they are, the Eds," Buddy What's-His-Name would say when they all met under the marquee on Saturday nights, Buddy and June, the other two, out for dinner in town and a movie;

Ed and Edna just a movie after dinner at home with the children. Jones? Johnson? Edna remembered their last name started with a J, but that was all. The peppermints kept Edna from coughing, and too, she remembered now while Dorothy waited, while she hummed and pulled the sticking plastic off the striped disc and popped it in her mouth, it made Buddy's tongue taste cool. Taste sweet.

Buddy?

"Come," Davie said. Moving day.

"Ma, I'm coming in," Dorothy said, now.

Edna dropped the brown purse and a copper bead detached and rolled over the floorboards. "No," Edna said, to the bead, to her daughter. Dorothy turned the dining room doorknob and shoved, but there was too much stuff. Too much to push through. Edna didn't use that door anymore.

"Come," Davie had said, Edna remembered, and she rose, finally, to her feet and followed her crying little boy out of the kitchen and through the dining room and into the foyer where the boxes were no longer piled impossibly high but fallen, scattered: broken vases and tea towels and record albums, and heaps of things and cardboard.

"Dorothy," Davie said, "sister." And Edna felt that heat she sometimes felt when her daughter did something wrong, did something stupid (coaxed Davie to jump with her from the roof of the garage, ate toothpaste until she threw up on the new shag bathmat, left the iron face down on a tablecloth so the linen burned black while she went to answer the phone on the wall in the kitchen).

"Dorothy!" Edna yelled. The heat filled her throat.

"Ma, I can't get in here. Please. We have to go."

It sounded like her daughter's mouth was right up against the door, the words sounded hard. Like wood. Like door.

"All right, all right," Edna said. She pulled her car coat (gray, dove gray, Buddy said it made her eyes look like river stones) off the coatrack and slid her arms into the sleeves. It was too large for her now. When had she become so small?

Dorothy had not come when Edna called, back then, moving day, and Edna went to the front door, pushed open the screen. "No," Davie said, and he grabbed the rear pocket of her Levi's, pulled. He slapped the heap of boxes. "Dodo," he said.

People always thought Davie was big for his age, two years younger than Dorothy, Dodo. But he wasn't. He was average. Average-sized. Below average in other ways. "Dumb for his age," Ed used to say, making a joke of it, just teasing, he'd say. But Edna's eyes stung whenever he'd say it, no matter how true. They hadn't known how hard the birth was, because no one did in those days. Out cold, thank God, and Ed in the waiting room or up the road in a tavern, waiting. Hours. By the time Edna woke up, Davie was down the hall with the others, the criers, and she was too sore, too tired to go see him just yet, so she didn't know he wasn't crying. That he hadn't yet, not much. She didn't know about her cord around his throat, about his blue skin. By the time she would let them wheel her down the hall, he was pink and beautiful and asleep, his small mouth an O, a perfect O, his little hands curled like seashells she'd only seen pictures of in books.

After Ed died, Edna thought she might travel.

After Ed died, Edna never went anywhere.

She put her hand in the pocket of her too-big gray car coat and felt something, and there they were. Her keys. There.

"Found them," she said. But then she felt something else. She had to pee.

Edna had smelled that sharp odor and she knew what it was. Near her feet in the foyer on that hot, hot moving day a small puddle formed. Davie's shorts went from pale blue to dark, his legs, strong boy calves covered in blond down like his father's, were wet.

"Here," Davie had said, hammering on the boxes, oblivious to his own piss, "here."

"Shit," Edna muttered. "Oh shit.

"Dorothy," Edna said. Then. Now. "Dodo!" And she felt something rise up in her chest, felt it boil in her throat. "Dorothy!"

"Ma, it's okay," Dorothy said from somewhere close. "I'm here, Ma, right here."

There was noise. Scrabbling and scraping, Edna heard the sounds in the foyer. She remembered digging in the boxes, looking, looking. She went to the dining room door now, the one with the junk in front of it, the boxes and bags and papers and clothes and broken things and unopened packages with colorful mailing labels, the things she liked to buy, order and receive, and she dug again. Now. Her throat was thick with dust, the smell of old things, of cheap things, of forgotten things, of unused things, of discarded but kept things. And fear. "Dorothy!"

"Here I am, Ma, it's okay, Ma." Dorothy's voice sounded calm—how could that be?—she sounded fine.

She'd been asleep, too, not Edna, but Dorothy, and not now, but way back then, moving day then, too darn hot day then, asleep under the boxes. She'd climbed into the spaces between them, hiding from Davie like she did, like he liked, until he didn't. If it took him too long to find her, he got frightened. He didn't like to be alone; he slept with the lights on. Poor, big little boy. Scared. And he and Edna had dug through the boxes to where he knew Dodo was, he'd seen her leg through the spaces between the boxes, but when he tried to reach her, to tug on her ankle, the pile of boxes fell. "Like pickup sticks," he said, when he told Ed later what happened because Edna made him, when Ed gave him a few good smacks for misbehaving, even though it was Dorothy really, who was to blame. It was usually Dorothy, Edna knew, the apple of her daddy's eye, daddy's girl. "Let's misbehave." Had Edna really heard her say that once to Davie, sweet Davie, dumb Davie, Davie who did whatever his big sister said?

"Ma?" And Dorothy was there now, her big, middle-aged face not quite inside but a slice where the dining room door pushed open an inch. She looked to Edna now like she had on moving day, sleepy and blinking, "Mommy?" Full of wonder. What's going on? What? Edna reached her fingers through the door. Were they her fingers? They looked so different from what she thought they looked like. Blue veins and bumps. She touched her daughter's nose. Dorothy, middle-aged, big-faced Dorothy laughed. Like a girl. She sounded like a girl. Like Edna's girl.

"She's fine," Edna said, her fingers on her daughter's face. "Dodo's fine, Davie."

"Ma, Davie's gone," Dorothy said, quiet now, soft now. Her face was still just a slice, but Edna saw her daughter's lips moving, saw the rosy lipstick in the tiny lines that radiated from her lips. Radiated? Was that a word? Radio. Radius. Radicchio. Radial. Radiate. Radiant.

"Radiant," that's what Buddy said to her that time in the dark of the movie theater when the last of the credits rolled up the screen and June and Ed were already gone, out on the sidewalk in the still of the night smoking cigarettes, talking maybe, probably not, because they had so little in common, nothing to say to one another, waiting for Buddy and Edna (who had so much in common, watching the credits of the movie already over, reading books, playing jazz on Edna's piano together and singing. *It's de-lovely.* Buddy and June lived across the street, on the other corner of Cole and Porter).

"What," Edna said in the movie-dark theater. They tucked their knees toward one another so the others in their row could pass. They touched knees. Edna remembered that. She wouldn't forget that.

"Your smile," Buddy said. "It's radiant."

"Ma, can we go? The movie is starting soon."

Where was she? Where was she?

"A minute," Edna told Dorothy. That's what she said whenever she excused herself to go to the bathroom. "A minute," she'd said to Buddy after he called her smile radiant, after their knees touched, after he leaned forward close enough she could almost read the credits reflected in his brown eyes, after he kissed her, his tongue so pepperminty she saw red stripes behind her eyelids.

In the bathroom, Edna tried to gather herself. To pull it together. To sort it all out. She hummed. She peed and wiped (she remembered that at least, what she was supposed to do in this place) and when she rolled up the flopping sleeves of her car coat to wash her veiny, bumpy hands at the sink (remembering that, too) she looked out the window to the street below. Dorothy's car. That big black thing that was more than a station wagon, but not quite a truck. An SU-something or other. Pulled up to the curb like it was for the first time in a long, long time those few months ago sometime after Dorothy had left her husband, left the city, left the country, then come back to town, come back home. Beyond the car, the street signs. Cole and Porter. Buddy and June's house in need of a paint job, a chain link fence around the front yard where those people who lived there now—who were they? Edna could not remember. Where were they from? Edna could not remember. Where were Buddy and June? Edna didn't have a clue—kept their huge, barking dogs. June had had a rose garden. And there was no fence. Edna watched from this very window when Buddy would come outside and scatter wet coffee grounds over the flower bed. Saturdays. Daylight. He wore his undershirt. She saw the morning shadow on his neck. Sometimes she could hear him whistling.

"I've got you under my skin." That's what Buddy had said to her in the dark movie theater while their spouses smoked on the sidewalk outside and after he'd said her smile was radiant and after he'd kissed her. And she said, "A minute." And got up from her seat, felt his knee rub along the side of her calf when she stood, stumbled just a little in the dark and down the steps from the balcony (they always sat in the balcony because that's where June liked to sit, far-sighted and prone to motion sickness if they got too close to the screen) and out of the auditorium to the bathroom. She locked the door behind her. She always locked the door behind herself.

Edna fumbled with the lock now. Dorothy had come all the way in the house, she heard her down there in the living room, she'd come in through the living room door. She wasn't supposed to come in. When Dorothy had moved back to town but refused to move back into her old bedroom, Edna, a little disappointed, a little mad, had made her promise she wouldn't come into the house unless she was invited. Edna was ashamed of how her house looked now, of the state it was in. She had been ashamed for a long time.

"Ma? Ma? Mommy?"

When Davie died, Edna went into a domestic frenzy and Ed took a new position that put him on the road three weeks every month. And Edna—stuck at home with her frantic grief that kept her scrubbing floors and washing windows and changing the sheets every two days and cooking pots of things she ladled into Tupperware and shoved into the already packed freezer—was stuck at home with her least favorite child, her teenaged daughter who had, herself, gone somewhere, not away, but gone wild, out late every night, sometimes all night. Night and day, sometimes.

"Coming," Edna said from the top of the stairs. She saw Dorothy's boots, not snow boots, it was just autumn after all, but dressy, shiny boots with zippers and heels, among the stuff that packed into the spaces of the living room. Edna watched, as she descended the steps, her daughter's boots become legs, become hips, become belly, become boobs, become neck, become head. Big face. Rosy lips. Silver hair. Her daughter had silver hair. Her child. Her baby.

Only, Davie was the baby.

He'd been born with a broken heart. They didn't know it then, like they didn't know about the difficult birth. They wouldn't know it for years until Davie was nearly a teenager and he would get tired easily, had trouble catching his breath sometimes. Doctors. More doctors. Finally, the diagnosis. A defect. Congenital. And Edna felt the guilt of that, her baby's inheritance. From her, maybe. Probably. Because Ed was strong. Healthy. (When, years later, in a motel room on the road selling insurance policies to big companies, Ed died at fifty-five of a faulty heart, too, it might have been a comfort to Edna, a kind of relief. Perhaps it should have been, but it wasn't. By then, her guilt had burrowed and settled even deeper than her sorrow.)

Right there, right where Dorothy stood in her shiny boots and silver hair, is where Edna had stood when she got the news about Davie. She'd come home from the hospital for just an hour, maybe two, long enough to jump in the shower, long enough to change her clothes, and yes, she'd wanted to nap, but just for a few minutes, she'd been up all night and the night before when they'd taken Davie in because he'd stood up from the dinner table and fallen down, right down, there in the dining room where those bags of newspapers were now, those unopened packages, where the pile of coats was, where Edna had tossed the purses (how long ago?) when she was looking for her keys. And there on the floor (right there, right there) he'd gone in and out, conscious and not, and so they took him to the hospital on the other side of the river, the big hospital, the good one. And he was alive then, and hooked up to machines, and that was good, wasn't that good? Edna remembered asking Ed that while they sat in hardbacked chairs in a waiting room down the hall from where Davie was alive, where Davie was hooked up to machines, "That's good, isn't it?"

"Good?" Dorothy tilted her silver-haired head, she pursed her rosy lips. "Ma, isn't what good?"

The tele-thing rang. Television. Telescope. Telegram. Telephone. Yes, that's it: telephone. On the wall just inside the swinging door of the kitchen, where it always was, where it always had been. Where it always rang. And where, sometimes now, especially late, late in the still of the night when Edna had finished her can of peas, her saltines and margarine, it would ring and Edna would answer and there would be a voice on the other end of the line, and static, and the voice, quiet, kind, would say "Edna? M'dear? Edna? That you there?" And she would say, yes, yes it was. And it felt good to answer the phone on those nights, the taste of peas still in her mouth, the slip of margarine on the very tips of her fingers; it felt good to hear that voice she'd come to know, low and quiet, kind. "Oh what a day I've had, my Edna, m'dear," he would say. And she'd say yes again, and he would tell her about his day (university and work and his sick, sick mother) in that voice that sounded so familiar but so, so different. Foreign. British, maybe. He would tell her and she would listen and when he took her credit card number again and again and again (because each card was rejected eventually, one after the other, she didn't know why, she was sorry, she was embarrassed) he confirmed her address like he had it memorized: "110 W. Cole. At the corner of Cole and Porter," and he would sing a little into the phone, into her ear, "It's delightful, it's delicious, it's de-lovely."

The telephone rang again.

"Ma?" Dorothy said. "Should I answer that, Mommy?" But Edna could tell that her daughter didn't want to answer the phone, she didn't want to move, it looked like, the way she frowned and studied the things on the floor by her feet, by the couch, by the door, the things she would have to climb over to get to the kitchen, the things she would have to push out of the way to open the door, all those things in her way.

The telephone stopped ringing. It was like the time Edna came home from the hospital, Davie still there, Davie still out of it. (Where was Dorothy then? Edna could not remember. Where was Ed?) And the phone rang but before she could answer it, it stopped. Then it started again, a minute later, no time at all, and Edna grabbed it off its hook and there was Ed, Ed on the phone, and his voice sounded like it always did, only not like that, he was crying, he never cried, but he was crying, sobbing and gulping and Edna sank to the floor (like on moving day, on the floor near the cupboards) and Davie was gone.

The day of the funeral was a hot one, too. Like moving day, like other days she could remember and not. Summer days and autumn days and spring days when the sky was clear and the sun was high and there was no wind. Too darn hot. And after, people came over to the house because that is what people did, Edna did not know why, she never could understand why, leave me alone, she wanted to tell them all. Let me be. But they came over and they sat on her couch and on her dining room chairs (like Davie did before he fell) and stood in her kitchen and there was food, lots of food, but Edna did not know (now or then) where the food had come from. It was so darn hot she thought she might melt. She wished she would.

"A minute," Edna said to someone, someone, another someone in a line of someones who said they were sorry, so sorry, who stood close but looked over her shoulder when they said they were sorry, looked at the wall or at someone else, looked anywhere, at any someone but Edna who (she knew, she knew) must have been hideous with her grief. Who would want to look at her, who would want to see that? "A minute," she'd said.

The bathroom was dark then because the shade was down on the window over the sink. Dorothy must have been in there because she was modest like that, teenaged and private. Full of shame (and desire, Edna knew, having caught her daughter more than once in the front seat of a boy's car in the still of the night). On that funeral day Edna stood in the middle of the dark room, not needing to be there but needing to be away from where she had been, downstairs where Dorothy stood now in her shiny boots and silver hair, downstairs where everyone else was, whispering, tsking.

But not everyone. Buddy at the door. (She hadn't locked the door.) Buddy in the bathroom. Buddy over the tiles and holding Edna before she fell, woozy with despair.

"Are you ready, Ma? The movie," Dorothy said. Her daughter's voice was gentle now, not hard like at the door a little while (how long?) ago. "Are you all right, Mommy?"

After Davie was gone and Ed was never there, they, Dorothy and Edna, yelled more than talked. They screamed. The things they said! Edna could not remember all of it. Not all the words, but she remembered—and this felt like a toothache, dull and throbbing—the way they hurt, the things they said to one another. The things she did remember, the things they screamed. "Whore!" Edna shrieked more than once, "tramp!" "Who, Ma?" Dorothy screamed back. "Who are you talking about?"

Buddy was there in the bathroom on the funeral day, catching Edna and holding her, letting her kiss him like she wanted, like she needed, letting her grab and move his hands up under her dress, touch her skin, warm her (even though it was hot, she was hot, she needed this warmth, his warmth) and press against her. Nothing happened, though, not really. Not what Edna had wanted, had needed, Buddy under her skin, Buddy inside her because there was space then (and now)—space that Davie had left behind, space that Ed never took up, space that needed filling. But Buddy, brown-eyed, peppermint-tongued Buddy who touched her knee with his when they sat close in the balcony of the movie theater (June on his other side) and who sometimes sang Cole Porter to her when they were alone watching credits ("delightful, de-lovely") was an honorable man. More or less. Honorable enough to pull away that funeral day, Edna's hideous grief day, honorable enough to say no, no, not this, you don't want this, even though Edna was pretty certain that she did. Honorable enough to pull away just in time, because Dorothy was there, too, on the landing, on the other side of the bathroom door that wasn't locked, and then inside the bathroom and crying, crying. Looking up from the crying and seeing Edna, seeing Buddy. Seeing.

It was too darn hot in her car coat and Edna felt dizzy. "Oh dear, oh dear," she said, and her knees dipped.

"Mommy," Dorothy said, and Edna recognized her little girl under the silver hair, saw the confusion in Dodo's eyes (gray like river stones, like her mother's) that was there on moving day when Edna and Davie had unburied the sleeping girl from beneath the moving boxes, there when Edna flew at her daughter back then, that day, her fear gone to relief gone to anger. There when her daughter curled into a corner of the foyer in the new old house, crying; Davie, crying too, patting his sister's arms, her cheeks, those places where the blows had landed, "Shh, Dodo," Davie said, "shhh." And that—for some awful, ungodly reason—had only made Edna madder. "You, Davie," and she yanked him from his sister's side, pointed toward the basement, pushed him toward the stairs, "your father will take care of you," she said. And Ed had. Edna remembered this. She didn't like to remember this, but she did.

Edna felt bad. She felt bad. Sick. Bad.

"Mommy?" Dorothy said again. "Mommy, are you all right? Mommy, should we sit?"

Dorothy cleared a space on the couch, pushed papers and clothing and parcels to the floor. She helped her mother out of the soft gray car coat, settled her amidst the stuff piled on the cushions. She tossed the coat over the back of a chair and the keys fell out of a pocket, jangled to the floor. Dorothy moved through things, things, and other things and into the kitchen. There was more there, on the table, on the counters; towers of empty vegetable cans stacked on the window sill, unopened packages greasy with fingerprints stood in piles on the kitchen floor, filled the sink. Dorothy read the labels. *Giftorama.* Return address post office box numbers, somewhere in New Jersey. On the brown paper wrapping of one of them, of two, of three, Dorothy saw her mother's name handwritten: *Edna.* And *M'dear* circled with red-crayoned hearts.

Dorothy filled a teacup (it was all she could find in the cupboards, besides more brown paper packages with red-crayoned hearts) with water from the tap, and blinking, gulping, she drank it down. She filled it again, drank some more.

When Dorothy was in Paris after her divorce, she met a man. She thought about him now. He was homeless, she was certain. He stood, morning and evening, at the end of the street where she was staying; or, sometimes she saw him in a chair in the corner of the laundromat in the middle of the block, dozing, maybe, or reading a paper through cracked glasses. A good-looking man, though. A pleasant face. Black. Her age or so, his long dreadlocks shot through with silver, a shuffle to his walk that looked like his hips hurt, like hers did after a long day of sightseeing, a short night on the hard futon in her vacation rental. The man had things. Possessions. Neat stacks of them pushed against the wall. Big, plastic bags stuffed with papers and magazines, clothes or rags. Rolling carts with their canvas bags cinched closed over whatever stuff was in them. Two yoga mats. Empty plastic bottles with brand names that were familiar to her (Coca Cola, Sprite) and not (Lorina, Lactel). His gathering of things took up an outside wall of a building, one quarter of the short block. There were occasions when the things weren't there on the street, and the first time Dorothy noticed that they weren't, she felt a small emptying inside, a sort of longing. Where were they? Where was he? Around the corner though, she saw him, arranging his things again, covering them all with flattened cardboard boxes and plastic garbage bags, blue tarps. Dorothy came to know his rhythm: this side of the street, morning and evening, around the corner in the middle of the day. It was a considerable task, she discovered watching him once from a table in the café across from her rental. Carrying and restacking, pieces at a time. It took hours. He whispered with himself as he worked. Sometimes he whistled.

Everyone seemed to know this man. In a country that prided itself on not inviting unwanted attention by staying stone-faced in public (an aging hippie tour guide she had met her first Paris day and slept with on her third, called this the "Metro Face" and sitting up in her tiny rental, his back against her only pillow, demonstrated by straightening the lines of his lips and his eyebrows, by staring blankly ahead), this gathering man was a smiler. A greeter. Bon jour, he said when he caught an eye in the morning, bon soir, as the sun went down. He traded handshakes and pleasantries with young men passing, white men in good shoes and fitted jackets, briefcases swinging at their sides. Said salut to the children on their scooters or running to and from the primary school a few blocks away. Nodded at the women who nodded back. Even she, Dorothy, a foreigner who, despite weeks in this city, despite the one-night stand with her guide that she had entered into whole-heartedly, still was wary of French strangers, of men of color especially (although she did not want to be), nodded and answered bon jour or bon soir, depending. Sometimes she even said it first.

And it was those times, when she passed the gathering man and the familiar comfort of his possessions in the street and willed him to look her way, when she smiled her big, Midwestern American smile and he returned it, that she felt happiest in Paris. She did not know that then—although in those moments she recognized the lifting behind her breastplate, the clearing of the semi-darkness of loneliness she thought then was a solo traveler's unexamined emotion, but understood later was something she carried with her to Paris and carried home again—but now, at her mother's sink in her childhood house at the corner of Cole and Porter, Dorothy understood that the times when she warmed with the memories of her trip to Paris (the glittering Eiffel Tower at dusk, the scent of fresh-baked bread everywhere, the buzz of a language around her she didn't understand but still somehow loved), it was this memory of the gathering man and his things that warmed her the most.

Dorothy filled the tea cup a third time, all the way up to its delicate rim. She pushed the kitchen door open and there was Edna on the couch among her stuff, eyes closed, rocking, humming.

"That's pretty, Mommy," Dorothy said, and Edna opened her eyes. "That's nice."

The mother smiled at her daughter. Dorothy held the teacup in both hands and went back to Edna, moving forward slowly, slowly. Stepping carefully now, carefully through the stuff and junk of her mother's life.

Acknowledgments

I have been gathering these stories for a long time now, and I have enjoyed the support of many during the process. For shelter, time, and all sorts of sustenance, I am grateful to Ragdale Foundation, Interlochen Center for the Arts, and Judy's Macatawa cottage.

My Columbia College Chicago family of students, mentors, and colleagues keeps me inspired and engaged. Thanks to Her Chapter, a bevy of Chicago women writers with whom I have shared ideas and resources, cheers and challenges. Thank you to Kim Suhr and Christi Craig, two wonderful Wisconsin writers and teachers who have welcomed me into their community, where I discovered Cornerstone Press.

My work finds its best way in the company of my writing getaway gal pals, Kathleen Quigley, Jana Dawson, and Doro Boehme (in memoriam), and the Wild Herons, Gail Wallace Bozzano, Anne-Marie Oomen, Julia Poole, Nancy Parshall, and Bronwyn Jones. Thank you as well to Katey Schultz and Christine Maul Rice, who provide the best writing communities.

I am crazy grateful to Dr. Ross Tangedal, Colin Aspinall, Tara Sparbel, Brianna Stumpner, Claire Hoenecke, and the rest of the crew at Cornerstone Press for helping me make a better book than I brought to them. And to Sheryl

Johnston, publicist, long-time friend, and colleague, thank you, and I am honored to work with you on this project.

Versions of a number of these stories first appeared in a variety of journals and publications. "What Was To Come," *101 Words;* "My Mother's Daughter," *Solstice Literary Magazine* (fiction first prize winner); "Things You Know But Would Rather Not," *American Fiction, Best Unpublished Stories by Emerging Writers;* "Good News Or Money," *Flyleaf;* "Tommy On The Roof," *Curbside Splendor e-zine;* "What Girls Want," *Barrelhouse Magazine;* "Good Men and Bad," *HairTrigger 2.0;* "Regarding Alix," *New Plains Review;* "Kitty," *Goreyesque;* "The Truth Is Not Much Good," *Solstice Literary Magazine;* "A Good Reader," *Between The Covers;* and "Maria Concepción," *Hyptertext Magazine.* Thank you to the publishers and editors for giving my words their first home.

Thanks to the McNairs, especially Don, Allen, and Kim. And to Maggie Hartigan and Anna Idol.

Finally and always, I am grateful for the support and encouragement from my first and best reader, my love, Philip Hartigan.

Afterword

In Praise of Silence, Loneliness, and Boredom

Now we will count to twelve
and we will all keep still.
-Pablo Neruda, "Keeping Quiet"

They gave me a tiny cabin in the woods. Living room, bedroom, kitchen, and bath. No TV. Spotty internet over a dial-up connection, long distance. I am a Chicago girl who was invited to be Writer-in-Residence at Interlochen Arts Academy, a remarkable high school with boarding and day students from all over the world, students with jaw-dropping talents. Music, theatre, art, filmmaking, dance. Writing. Autumn into winter, short, dark days in Northern Michigan. Quiet. Quiet. Quiet. Silence, really.

I was a little terrified.

My regular Chicago life at the time was two trips a day on the CTA, chatter and noise all around me, sirens and engines and other people's television sets on too loud in the building next to me—our windows less than a foot from one another—an apartment that was never dark because the streetlights from outside streamed in through the blinds and the curtains. Cars drove up and down the street in front of that building all day and night, a huge dog in the apartment above me always barked when his people weren't home, and barked even more when his people were. Our place was underneath the flight pattern for jets coming into O'Hare from over the lake.

I didn't know silence. I didn't even know quiet very well. But soon enough, in my cozy rooms with wood-paneled walls and orange shag carpet that held the sand tracked in from beneath the trees, in this space that smelled like summer camp, smelled of forests and bug spray, I got over my fear of silence, of disconnecting. After just a few days, I felt myself yearning toward the velvet quiet.

Then, a week after I arrived and on the first day of classes at Interlochen, September 11, 2001, the World Trade Center was attacked.

Talk about noise.

When I walked through the lanes on campus and under the trees behind the cabins and dorms, I could see the blue flicker of television in the students' common lounges; I could hear phones ringing from inside the buildings; I could see through their windows, people huddled together talking furiously and sadly. I could hear, I swear, that strange mechanical sound of internet connections made over phone lines, the small bong and screech of them.

Back in my own cabin, though, without a television, with limited internet access, I could hear nothing. I could turn it all off. I did have a radio, and I will be forever grateful to Interlochen Public Radio for its news, for its level-headed reporting. It kept me updated on what I needed to know, when I felt I needed to know it. But when I turned off the radio, like I did for most hours of every day, the silence that filled my cabin allowed me to pay close attention to the story unfolding, to the humanness of it, to the emotional pull of our country's narrative as it developed over those weeks, those months. In the quiet I could, in fact, listen deep.

I seldom went out then except to teach, to grab a few provisions, to run by myself near the lakes and the wetlands. I never have been more lonely than I was during that time. More immersed in silence, more deeply distracted by my own thoughts, more prone to wallowing in my own self-imposed disconnection and boredom.

I also never have written more than I did during those five months.

I was drawn to "an inward silence," as Terry Tempest Williams calls it: "a howling silence that brings us to our knees and our desk each day." Quiet and stillness lead me to the page, like Terry Tempest Williams also said, "Silence is where we locate our voice."

We know this about silence, I think, and yet, we continue to allow ourselves to be taken out of the silence we crave, the silence we need. The silence our work needs. We compose on a computer because we tell ourselves we type faster than we can hand write—as though this were a good thing, writing faster. And the clack of the keys disturbs the silence in a way no whispering scratch of a pen on paper can. We keep the internet in the palm of our hand now so we can look things up whenever we need to, or at least tell ourselves that (I need to, I need to) as we let go of a sentence in progress because our phones have buzzed, or we really, really must see right this instant if we got a response to that email or how many people liked the photo of our cat we posted on Facebook this morning.

Even now, as I write this, I find myself shallowly distracted, caught up in the daily noise of my regular city life, even though now, today, we are in the desperate quiet of stay at home orders in the middle of a pandemic. Cars (fewer than usual) and sirens (louder in this unusual, relative quiet) run beneath my ninth-floor window. I want to check my email, to make a list of the things I should do today. I stop to listen to the bus on the street outside, its recording that calls out the route number and the intersection; was that my phone that just dinged? I want to see what the orange man in the white house tweeted this morning, I want to watch the news. I fight the pull of technology and 24-hour information, the lure of laundry and dishes, of student papers and of that lovely hunk of Australian cheddar cheese in the fridge. I am easily, shallowly distracted.

Still, despite my bad habits, I am a fan of distraction. Not the kind I just spoke of, that behavior that keeps us skimming on the surface of things, like humming birds, dipping and flitting, dipping and flitting. The distraction I yearn for, the kind I advocate for is something else. Deep distraction, born of quiet. That is what I want.

What I mean: I used to be a runner. For various reasons that include a new titanium hip, I no longer run. Instead, I would use one of those tedious machines at the gym—now closed, like the restaurant across the way where we enjoyed happy hour and our fellow regulars at its bar is now closed, like the bank and beauty shop and resale shop along the street are closed. When I used to run, and later when I could still use the machine, I never put on headphones or listened to music. I listened, instead, to the meanderings of my mind. I listened until (Terry Tempest Williams again) "in silence the noises outside cease so the dialogue inside can begin." I listened—I listen, here above it all closed up in our high rise apartment—deep, and allow (invite?) myself to be deeply distracted by the memories and questions and stories I carry with me always.

Like this: outside the window of the gym where I would sweat, teenagers would pass by on their way to school. There was always a group of girls and a group of boys, and in between the two groups there would be a couple, a boy and a girl, hands in one another's back pockets. When I was in junior high, I remember seeing that gesture for the first time. At the shopping center where I'd go to the Woolworth's to play with white, pink-nosed mice in their cages, I saw my next-door neighbor with a boy (she was sixteen) and he slid his hand into the back pocket of her jeans. That seemed so intimate and grown up to me, I yearned for that sort of closeness with a boy. What is it about those ages, thirteen, sixteen, that makes us so eager to be older? My brothers were all older than me, and getting into various sorts of trouble. Roger ran away with the carnival. Don would cut class some Fridays and have parties at our house while our folks were at work. Allen was unhappy and sometimes filled with such an acute sense of otherness that he first attempted suicide when he was just eighteen. Was this, our bad behavior (I ditched school a lot in high school, too, I took a lot of drugs, even though I was a good girl, in the drama club and the National Honor Society) connected to the fact that my father died when I was just fifteen, Roger seventeen, Don and Allen brand new adults? Maybe, I don't know. Perhaps. Let me write about that a bit. Let me see what I can figure out.

That is how it works for me.

I think of this . . .

That reminds me of this . . .

That makes me think of that . . .

And that reminds me of this . . .

And this, finally, moves my pen towards that.

If I had been on my machine with earbuds filling my head with Morning Edition or MSNBC or Fleetwood Mac or *This American Life*, I would not have been able to hear the progression of these deep, internal distractions.

You try:

Turn off the noise.

Think of something you saw this morning or yesterday or this week or sometime recently. Let yourself see the thing, the moment, the interaction, in your mind. Recreate the image.

What does it remind you of? Think about it for a minute. Tell it to yourself in your head. Speak it through. Now what does that remind you of?

And that makes you think of . . . what?

Don't write, not just yet. Look. Listen. Tell.

And when the pull of the words, the images, the moments is too strong to resist, when it leads you to the page, follow it. Write. Write. Write.

Arundhati Roy tells us "Another world is not only possible, she is on her way. On a quiet day, I can hear her breathing." This gives me comfort right now, in this superbly messed up time in our history. Further, to my mind, that is a good summation of this practice of deep distraction. The other world is on her way, listen. Listen deep.

Here is something else I believe about silence and deep distraction: in this quiet and intense internal listening, I can discover resonance. The moments from my memories, my work, what I've read, what I've seen—those moments, emotions, and bits of life that come back to me again and again resonate for me. In some cases, these are the things

I might try to ignore, to forget, to drown out. The pain of my past, the ache of loss, the odd moments that have left me vulnerable in my sadness or even, sometimes, in my elation. When I am quiet, I can hear the resonance of those things, too.

Marianne Moore reminds us in her poem "Silence" that "the deepest feeling always shows itself in silence." And while this deep feeling might make me (us) uncomfortable at times, the creative possibilities in what resonates in the silence are essential. Henry David Thoreau said "If we will be quiet and ready enough, we shall find compensation in every disappointment."

But for me, perhaps for you, too, silence is hard to come by. Even if I do the things that invite it—turn off the radio in the car, drive in the quiet; leave the television dark for an extra hour or two each day; turn off my phone; leave my earbuds in my bag; write with a pen that whispers over the page; listen to my thoughts, my memories, my questions, my stories—even if I do all of this, there is still noise and bustle around me. Even now, when there should be more quiet than not, when we are supposed to be behind our own doors, when we are asked not to gather and go. My next challenge then, is to cultivate my internal listening even as I am interrupted by the external noise. I will be part of this hubbub if I must (talking too loudly to the faces on my computer, listening to the birds in the trees) but while I am, I will try to use what I hear, I see, I notice, and let my stories and sentences and essays develop in my mind. I will talk to myself (maybe not out loud, but if so, quietly. Maybe just breath and lips moving) and tell myself the lines, the scenes, the stories I hear inside. I will mine these moments of life's distractions for possibilities at the writer's desk.

Some writers say you need to live an active and engaged life in order to have something to write about. And for some, that might be true. But what if an active and engaged life keeps me from moments of exquisite solitude, from the rich and nourishing states of loneliness?

Henry Miller was a proponent of loneliness: "An artist is always alone," he said, "…what an artist needs is loneliness." And Henry Rollins said this: "Loneliness adds beauty to life. It puts a special burn on sunsets and makes night air smell better." I believe this.

Here's something more I know about loneliness. Years have passed since my time at Interlochen, since I returned to my noisy life in my noisy city. I have an attentive husband and friends and students and colleagues, so I don't ever need to feel lonely. But some of my loneliest moments are the most fruitful to me as a writer. When I am lonely—and I can be lonely in a crowd, feel apart, feel other (don't most writers feel some sense of otherness?)—when I feel lonely, I look and listen inward. I listen deep to claim my own ground, to establish my own presence. This, I believe, is where my best writing comes from. Loneliness makes for good writing.

And then there's loneliness's fraternal twin, boredom. Boredom is often a form of resistance, I know; it can stand in the way of pushing through to the good work.

Sometimes I work on a piece through a couple of drafts, make it good and then better, and then, when the real work is on me, the push through to making it as best I can, I am apt to say, "I'm tired of this." I am apt to sit back in my chair, turn on my phone. I am apt to flip through headlines and posts, to say, "I'm bored." It would be so easy to set the piece aside now, letting it be forever better, but never best. But in order to get to my best, I must push through the boredom until the work becomes something new, something fresh. Don't most things take some struggle to get to the next level? (I am not just talking about writing here.) I understand, too, when I feel the boredom pulling me away from the desk, that it is just a defense mechanism, a way of keeping me from the work that is not only hard, but potentially complex and painful, risky perhaps, yet interesting and ultimately satisfying. Boredom pretends that it is saying, "quit, give up, change course." Really, though, it is whispering, "don't quit, make it better, listen closely, try this, follow the tangents, explore the distractions, make a leap, take the risk."

Now I will count up to twelve
and you keep quiet and I will go.
-Pablo Neruda, "Keeping Quiet"

In my light and noise-filled apartment in the city, just like on those dark, post-9/11 mornings in my cabin in the woods, I yearn toward the velvet quiet. It's there, no matter how loud the world may seem. I can hear it breathing. No matter my loneliness, my boredom, the levels of my distraction, I can hear, too, when I listen deep, this: "Write, damn it. Write."

March 2020, from *Hypertext Magazine*